THE TROUBLE WITH PERFECT

THE
TROUBLE
WITH
PERFECT

MARY E. RYAN

Simon & Schuster Books for Young Readers

SIMON & SCHUSTER BOOKS FOR YOUNG READERS
An imprint of Simon & Schuster Children's Publishing Division
1230 Avenue of the Americas
New York, New York 10020
Copyright © 1995 by Mary E. Ryan
SIMON & SCHUSTER BOOKS FOR YOUNG READERS is a
trademark of Simon & Schuster
Designed by Diane DePasque
The text of this book is set in Baskerville
Manufactured in the United States of America
First Edition
10 9 8 7 6 5 4 3 2 1
Library of Congress Cataloging-in-Publication Data
Ryan, Mary E.
        The trouble with perfect / by Mary E. Ryan.
            p.   cm.
            Summary: Thirteen-year-old Kyle, who is hopeless in
math, is tempted to cheat on an exam to please his demanding,
heavily drinking father.
            [1. Self-esteem—Fiction. 2. Fathers and sons—Fiction.
            3. Alcoholism—Fiction. 4. Honesty—Fiction.] I. Title.
            PZ7.R955Tr 1995
            [Fic]—dc20
            94-25745
            CIP
            ISBN : 0-689-80276-5

For J. Z.

CHAPTER 1

I opened one eye and looked at Rowena.

"I've got a great idea. Let's run away!"

Rowena Whipple frowned. "What on earth for?" she asked. "What do you have against Wheaton?"

"It's dinky and boring," I said. "And that's just for starters."

She shot me a glance. "Some people," she said, "are impossible to please. Besides, Wheaton isn't dinky—it's peaceful!"

It was Saturday, the last weekend of summer. Rowena lay on her back, eating peanuts. I was sprawled next to her in the Whipples' front yard. I rolled over and watched an ant crawl up my arm. But I wasn't thinking about ants, or eating peanuts, or what a boring, peaceful place Wheaton was.

I was thinking about secrets.

Well, *one* secret in particular. But I wasn't about to tell Rowena.

Of course, some things you can't keep secret. Take height, for instance. At the ripe old age of thirteen it's tough to admit you've reached the grand total of sixty inches. Five-foot zip.

It's even tougher when half the girls in your class can look down and count every hair on your head. Not to mention that your older brother, the Wheaton, Pennsylvania, slam-dunk champion, still calls you "Squirt" every chance he gets (and he gets a lot of chances).

On the other hand, if anyone else tried to call me "Squirt," Brian would leap to my defense. And I mean leap, because he slam-dunked a couple of friends who tried it. Bri isn't big on secrets. You know where you stand with him, and that's that.

Then again, secrets are hard to keep in a town like Wheaton.

"It's like living in a huge blender!" I told Rowena. "Everybody knows what everybody else is thinking. How's a person supposed to stand out from the crowd in a place like this?"

"Most people don't want to, Kyle," Rowena answered. She sat up and tossed a peanut at a gray squirrel. He froze, overwhelmed by his good luck, then darted over to the nut and scampered away with it. "This town is the median average of everything. The point is to fit in, not to stand out."

"Great," I said. "So if this place is so average, what are *you* doing here?"

Rowena gave me a withering look and split a peanut shell between her teeth. We both knew what I was talking about.

You could use a lot of words to describe Rowena Whipple: smart, stubborn, loyal, sometimes obnoxious. But definitely not average.

She looks pretty normal, in a gawky, dark-haired, freckled kind of way. I studied Rowe's long, pale legs that were stuck out in front of her on the grass. With legs like those, I wouldn't be facing my yearly ordeal: getting kicked off the Wheaton Junior High basketball team.

Every fall for the last two years Coach Simpson had said the same thing: "Nice footwork, Maxwell. But let's wait in case you shoot up a little first. Then we'll see about getting you off the bench." Right, Coach. I'm sure I'll be shooting up any day now. Yup. Any day.

It wasn't like I was the only short kid in school. There were plenty of shrimps fumbling around with the ball. The problem was, I was the only one who had Brian Maxwell, the slam-dunk king of Wheaton High, for an older brother.

A peanut landed in my hair. "What's the matter with you?" Rowena frowned. "You sound like a leaky wind tunnel with all that sighing."

"Sorry." I shook the peanut into my hand and lobbed it back at her. "Just thinking about school." I sighed again.

"Ky-uhl." Rowena likes to give my name two syllables, especially when she's irritated. "It's only eighth grade, okay? Eighth grade is not that big a deal for most people. Why don't you relax?"

"That's easy for you to say," I grumbled. "You get

perfect grades. You're tall. Everybody likes you. You don't have any problems."

"I only get perfect grades in math, and that's because I was born being good at math. Anyway, you get good grades, too."

"But I have to kill myself to get them."

"Well, everybody likes you too, Kyle." I noticed she skipped the "tall" part. "You're a lot more popular than I am."

That one surprised me. "I am?"

"What are you, blind? Don't you see how the girls snicker and giggle and act stupid around you? That's because they like you."

And all this time I thought it was because I was five-foot zip. Then I pictured Celia Simkewicz. I tried to remember whether she'd ever acted stupid around me. I didn't think so; Celia was totally incapable of acting stupid.

"Well, you're a girl," I pointed out. "You don't know how tough it is."

Rowena barked out a hollow laugh. It sounded like "oh-ho-ho." "And just what would you know about being a girl?"

She had me there. "All I meant was you don't have to go around proving stuff to everybody. When's the last time you had to beat somebody up, just to save face?"

"I beat up the Rat all the time." The Rat was Arnold, Rowena's five-year-old brother.

"You do not beat up the Rat; you smack him on the rear end. As a matter of fact, I think he likes it," I said.

"Whatever." Rowena tossed back her hair, which was as straight as a stick and flew around her face like uncooked spaghetti. "You have no idea what it's like to be a girl, Ky-uhl. It's plenty tough."

"It's a piece of cake," I said, just to make her mad.

It worked. She scrambled to her feet, jumped on my back, and started pummeling me across the shoulders. I let out a yelp, but she didn't let up. Her fists were incredibly hard; it felt like she was hitting me with a sock full of BBs.

On second thought, I decided, ducking away from the blows, maybe the Rat wasn't that crazy about his sister swatting him. I'd have to ask him one of these days.

"Say it!" Rowena yelled. I rolled away from her, and she came after me, launching a fresh attack. "Go on, say it!"

"Say what?" I gasped. "Uncle? Aunt?"

"No! Say, 'boys do not have it tougher than girls.'" She was on top of me now, crushing me with those long, noodly legs. Rowena Whipple was starting to remind me of a boa constrictor.

"Boys . . . tougher . . . girls." My lungs were about to collapse from the weight of her on my back.

"I can't hear you!"

"BOYS DO NOT HAVE IT TOUGHER THAN GIRLS!" I yelled.

I coiled my legs underneath me and then sprang up, pushing her off. "Jeez, Rowe," I said, brushing the peanut shells off my shirt. "You didn't have to take it so personally. What's the big deal?"

Rowena ignored me. She snatched up the bag of peanuts and started walking toward her house.

"Rowe? What's the matter? What did I say?"

"Nothing," she called over her shoulder.

I watched her go, feeling confused. It wasn't like I'd called her flat as a board, which was the truth. I hadn't pointed out that her face belonged on a cute, freckled monkey, which was also the truth. I hadn't even suggested that she do something with her hair, instead of letting it fall in her face all the time.

My shoulders hurt where her knuckles had dug into them. And she was still mad. Wasn't she?

"See ya, Rowena!" I yelled. For a second I didn't think she'd heard me. Then, at the front steps, she turned around and stuck her tongue out at me.

Whew. "Close one, Maxwell," I muttered to myself. I didn't just mean the Rowena attack. The fact was, I'd come this close to spilling my guts about Celia Simkewicz.

Not that Rowena would care. In fact, she might have given me some decent advice on the subject. But a secret is still a secret.

I was crossing the street when my brother's blue bike came hurtling past. The next minute I felt his hand on my head. I ducked.

"Wrestling girls again, Squirt?" Brian grinned. "Better watch it. Looked for a minute like the Rowena Monster had you pinned."

"She did not!"

"That's not the way our judges saw the match."

Whistling through his teeth, he sped past me toward the house. The next instant the whistling stopped.

I peered down the driveway, and then I understood why.

Dad was home.

CHAPTER 2

People say that Bri and I look alike, but I can't see it. His hair is dark and curly like Mom's, while mine is straight and light brown, with dull yellow patches here and there. Mom says Dad's hair was that color once, before the yellow turned to silver.

Brian's almost six feet tall and big through the shoulders; he's been shaving since he was a freshman. ("But the first year was just practice," he told me.) He's got bright blue eyes, and a quick fuse. In that one way, he takes after our dad.

I guess I'm more like my mom: I like to keep the peace. I don't think fighting solves anything unless you're a heavyweight contender with a big payday on the line. Yelling, shoving, hurting people's feelings—they just make things worse.

Bri says a person's got to fight for what he believes. I tried to tell him that there's different ways of fighting for what you believe, that don't involve yelling and stuff, but he just put me in a headlock and called me a wimp.

I followed his long legs up the front steps. He glanced

over at Dad's shiny blue Taurus parked in the driveway.

"Must have gotten back from Harrisburg early," he said.

Harrisburg is where my dad's company has its main office. He sells office fixtures—desks and chairs, credenzas and filing cabinets, cubicles and floor mats. Whenever Dad was in a good mood, he'd laugh and say how hard his job was, selling furniture to tight-fisted office managers, and call himself "Chair-Man of the Bored." That always got a big laugh out of us when we were younger. Nowadays he didn't say it as often, and when he did, we didn't laugh.

"Well, it's Saturday," I pointed out. "They probably didn't have a very long meeting."

"Good," Brian said, and pushed the door open.

The smell of brownies hit me the minute I got inside. On Saturdays my mom goes crazy with cooking and baking. The rest of the time she's too busy—she works for a real estate broker in Wheaton, showing houses and condos for sale.

"Hi," she called out when Brian and I reached the kitchen. The whole counter was covered with food. There were brownies cooling in the pan, and a meatloaf, and some kind of fruit bread, and a bunch of fresh vegetables she'd picked for a salad.

"Arrghh!" Brian started making ravenous gurgling sounds and lurching around the kitchen like the Hunchback of Wheaton. He leaned over Mom, his hands curled into claws. "Esmerelda,

Esmerelda!Argggh! Me want brownies! Brownnneees!"

Mom laughed and ducked away from him. "Oh, Bri, stop it! Your face will freeze like that. And don't touch those brownies. They'll ruin your appetite."

Brian straightened and winked at me. "They learn that one in a handbook, you know," he remarked, reaching past me to pry a warm brownie out of the pan. "The Motherhood Manual. 'Your face will freeze like that.' 'You'll poke your eye out.' 'No brownies before dinner.'"

"How about 'Wait an hour before swimming'?" I was getting into the spirit of the thing. Mom tried to swat Brian away from the food, but she looked like she was enjoying it too.

Brian waved his brownie at me. "No, I think that one has some scientific basis," he said. "Now, faces freezing..."

"Hey, there's always a first time," I said, and Brian and I held an impromptu face-distorting contest, while my mother giggled and pretended to look angry.

"What's all the ruckus about?"

My father stood in the doorway watching us. He was still wearing the white shirt and blue tie from his meeting, but his hair looked rumpled, as if he'd just gotten up from a nap.

After a moment he walked over to the refrigerator and took out a beer. Cracking open the can, he took a sip and then smiled at my mother. "Say, it smells great in here. What have you been doing, Bets? Cooking us out of house and home?

"Not really," my mother replied. "Just a few things for the week. A casserole, some goodies for the boys . . ."

"Aren't I one of the boys?" Dad said, as he came over to inspect the brownies.

"Yes," Mom said firmly, "and as I just told them, no sweets before dinner. Now scoot. Kyle, go wash your hands. You can help me with the salad. Bri, change out of those yucky things and put them in the hamper. Jim, why don't you take the dog out? She's been inside all day."

Obediently, the three of us trooped out of the kitchen.

"Just get in, Dad?" I asked him, as he made no move to locate Cindy, our seven-year-old cocker spaniel.

"A few minutes ago. I was unloading some wood in the garage. Saw one of those little roadside stands on the way back from Harrisburg. They had cords of firewood for sale, dirt cheap."

"Firewood?" Brian stared at him. "But it's still *summer*, Dad. It's hot out!"

Dad calmly sipped his beer. "It'll be cooling off soon enough. No harm in putting in an extra supply, is there?"

Brian shook his head, while the old tense feeling came over me again. Lately I'd been giving it a name: Referee Mode. Whenever Brian and Dad started bickering, I got this powerful urge to blow the whistle and send them to their separate corners. Before something happened.

Usually nothing did. So why did I have this tight, breathless feeling, like my lungs were filling up with water? I mean we were talking about *wood* here! Weren't we?

As quickly as the dangerous feeling hit me, it was gone. Brian clumped off to change out of his bike gear. Dad whistled for Cindy, who galloped creakily over to him, and I watched the two of them stroll out the door and across the lawn.

Just like nothing had happened, I thought. And nothing had. But when I got up to the bathroom, I closed the door and stood there for a long time, letting the cool water flow over my wrists, until Brian began pounding on the door, yelling that he wanted to take a shower.

During the summer we ate at the picnic table out on the patio. Every year Dad would stare at the yard and announce that next year, when he got a big order, he was going to put in a pool. "Won't that be great, guys?" he always asked, and even though the big order never seemed to come, we always told him that yeah, a pool would sure be great.

I finished two helpings of meatloaf, salad, and french fries, and then started on a pile of brownies. Brian was wolfing down the food too. But Dad sat back, rolling his beer can between his palms, hardly eating a bite.

Finally he put down the can and gazed around the table.

"I'd like your attention, guys. You too, Bets." I had half a brownie crammed in my mouth, but I swallowed it quickly.

My father isn't a big guy, not tall and rangy the way Brian is. But he was quite the athlete in college, and it still showed in the quick way he moved, and in how he looked at things. Survival, he said, meant staying one step ahead of the competition. And the way to do that, he'd add, was to make sure you were the best.

Now, even though he was flashing the old salesman grin, I had a weird feeling that the competition was starting to close the gap.

"I don't know how else to put this," he began, "but I'll get right to the point. We had a pretty rough meeting today. Sales haven't been so hot. Our team's done pretty well—I mean, how could they help it, with their three-time Salesman of the Year here—but overall, things are flat."

I glanced at Mom. She looked worried.

"The deal is that the company's streamlining its sales force. Downsizing, they call it. In plain English, that means there's going to be layoffs. Now, don't look at me like that. My job's not on the line. Yet. But . . . they had to let some people go. And they're bringing in a new supervisor to make sure the rest of us take up the slack."

Dad sighed. His hand closed around the empty beer can and crumpled it in one slow motion. "I just thought you all ought to know. I'm going to be putting in some long hours for a while, and there probably won't be a big bonus this year. So we're in for a little belt-tightening, folks."

"I could get a job after school, Dad," Brian said quickly. "Just until things pick up."

"Me too," I chimed in. "I could get my old paper route back, I bet."

"Hold it right there." Dad got up from the picnic table.

He began pacing up and down the patio flagstones. "No one's getting any jobs, okay? The biggest favor you boys can do is to stay on top of your homework. And your sports. That means you especially, Brian. In another year you'll be heading off to college, and I don't want you blowing your chance at a scholarship."

Brian looked down at the table.

"Is that understood?"

"Yes, sir," he mumbled.

"You too, Kyle. It's not too soon to think about getting your grades in shape. The good schools don't just look at your senior year, you know."

I stared at Dad. He was talking about college!

I remembered Rowena telling me not to sweat eighth grade, that it wasn't a big deal. Then again, she didn't have the Chair-Man of the Bored for a father.

Finally Dad turned to Mom.

"Betsy, I'm really sorry. I know you'd like to be home with the boys. Have more time for your artwork. I hoped it could be this year. But I know it won't take long to turn things around. Just hang in there, okay?"

Mom nodded, but her face was pale. I felt her hand settle on my shoulder and give it a squeeze.

"That goes for everybody in this family. We're all going to hang in there. We're a team, right?"

Dad was pulling out the old sales pep talk. Right then, I didn't really want to hear it—how we were a team, and we were all going to pull together, how when the going got tough, the Maxwells got going.

But I didn't have the heart to tell him. I kind of figured he needed to say it more than we needed to hear it.

He was still talking. "Now, I don't need to tell you that none of this gets repeated outside this house. There's enough folks who have problems; they don't need to hear about ours. Understood?"

Everyone nodded. When the going got tough, the Maxwells clammed up. That was the unspoken family rule—if there was a problem, we'd deal with it ourselves.

Dad went over to the cooler. I watched him take out another can of beer. Mom's eyes followed him too.

"Jim? You've hardly eaten a bite. You should eat something, honey. You've had a tough day."

Dad paused before cracking open the beer. Then he came over to the picnic table and kissed my mother on the cheek.

"You're right," he said. "Now, how about one of those killer brownies? Or do I have to clean my plate first?"

Brian and I laughed at that one. Even Mom smiled as she handed him the plate of brownies. He took two and passed the plate to me. But somewhere in the last ten minutes my appetite had vanished.

Maybe Dad's had too. Because when dinner was over, and we were clearing the table, those two brownies were still sitting there, untouched. I watched Mom gather them up and carry the plate inside.

I followed her into the kitchen. Dad was already in the living room, watching the sports channel. Brian was out in the driveway shooting baskets.

I looked at Mom. "Need any help cleaning up?"

She smiled. "I think I can handle it, Kyle. But thanks." She peered into my face. "Now, don't you worry about stuff. Everything's going to be just fine. You heard your dad just now. You take care of your schoolwork and leave the rest to us. Okay?"

I nodded. But when I went upstairs, I wasn't thinking about schoolwork. Instead, I reached for my headset and turned it up full blast. I didn't care what was playing, just something to drown out the noise in my head. But it didn't work.

What would happen if Dad lost his job? I couldn't imagine Dad driving an old car, or Brian not being able to go to college. I tried to picture living in a smaller house, or not having enough to eat, or wearing old clothes. But I couldn't. It was just . . . impossible.

I flipped the dial to another station. Cindy came trotting into the room. She flopped down next to my bed and I stroked her silky ears. Their golden color reminded me of Celia Simkewicz's shiny blond hair.

Cindy nudged my hand with her head and rolled her big brown eyes. I gazed into them for a long time, while a soft mushy song played on the radio and I thought about Celia.

Suddenly I jerked upright, and opened my notebook. What was the matter with me? I didn't even like mushy songs!

I grinned at Cindy.

"That's a good one, huh, girl?" I told the dog. "If Celia

Simkewicz only knew what she reminded me of—a cocker spaniel!"

Cindy looked flattered.

CHAPTER 3

By the end of the first day of school I knew three things:

1. I wasn't going to make the basketball team, again;

2. Celia Simkewicz was the prettiest girl in the eighth grade, if not North America; and

3. I hated Boyd Pearson's guts.

Then again, I had always hated Boyd's guts, ever since he'd started stealing my lunch in the third grade. For an entire year Boyd the Bully made off with my tuna fish and carrot sticks, my corn chips and cookies. It didn't stop until Mom found out I'd been eating Scott Kenyon's sandwiches instead of my own. (Scott's mom sold real estate too.)

Brian was outraged. "You mean that little creep Pearson has been taking your lunch, and you let him, Squirt?"

"He said he'd pound me," I blubbered.

"So pound him back!"

"He's bigger than I am." This was the truth. Boyd Pearson was built like a Tonka truck. An extremely hungry Tonka truck.

18

"Well, he's not bigger than your brother."

Sure enough, the next time Boyd showed up to claim my tuna fish, the reinforcements were there, in the form of Brian and his pal Smitty.

"Hungry, Pearson?" Brian asked. He stood over the table of trembling third-graders, arms folded like Superman's.

Boyd's pudgy face fell as he stared up at my big twelve-year-old brother. His hand, which was stretched out to grab my food, froze.

"What's the matter, fat boy?" Smitty taunted him. "Your mama doesn't make you a lunch?"

Brian reached over and caught Boyd's wrist. A quiet cheer of excitement spread around the table as Boyd began to whine and then moan. The arm-twisting continued until Mr. Hermanson, the assistant principal, came marching over to see what two seventh-graders were doing in the little kids' cafeteria.

Boyd skulked off, muttering threats under his breath, but that was the last sandwich he ever swiped. Unfortunately, it wasn't the last of Boyd Pearson.

Sure enough, when I reported to the gym for basketball tryouts, there was Boyd, bigger than life. He smirked when he saw me.

"Hey, Maxwell. Looks like you grew a whole millimeter over the summer."

I fixed him with an imitation of Rowena's withering stare. But it didn't wither Boyd. He was still big, but the pudginess was gone. Whatever he ate for lunch must be working. He towered over me.

"Very funny, Pearson," I answered. "A whole millimeter. Ha ha. That's hilarious."

"It's no joke, Kyle. It's the truth. You're such a shrimp you should start carrying around cocktail sauce."

At that point, Coach Simpson came out of the locker room, and made us line up in order of height. I had to admit that Boyd was right, except about the millimeter. I was now the shortest kid in the whole eighth grade.

"Okay, men. Let's see some action out on the court."

For the next half hour we dribbled and passed and shot. We scuttled in place until the gym was full of squeaking sneakers. We went one on one. Naturally I had to guard Boyd Pearson. That was a laugh. He rolled over me like a power mower.

At the end of tryouts I felt Coach Simpson's heavy hand on my shoulder. He peered down at me and frowned. "You eating right, Maxwell? Getting in your four basic food groups?"

I nodded, wondering if he was going to try to sell me some vitamin supplements.

The coach scratched his head. "Seems I recall that by your age your brother was already shooting up. Yep, if I remember, he'd already shot up quite a bit."

Coach Simpson's obsession with "shooting up" was getting on my nerves. All I could picture was Wyatt Earp or the Jolly Green Giant. Neither applied to me.

I shrugged. "I guess different people are on different shooting-up schedules, Coach."

He scratched his head some more. Then he fingered

the whistle hanging around his neck and squinted at me.

"What are you, about five-foot?"

I nodded.

"Maybe your mom should take you in for a checkup," he continued after a thoughtful pause. "Make sure the old thyroid isn't out of whack." He frowned again. "Couldn't hurt to find out."

I gazed at him steadily. "Maybe I should try a few steroids," I suggested. "I understand they can have a person shooting up practically over the weekend."

Coach Simpson's eyes bugged out. I could tell he was trying to decide whether I was a smart aleck or just plain stupid.

Finally he gave up and shook his head. "I know you don't mean that, son. And I don't blame you if you feel disappointed. But I just don't think we can start you this year, Kyle. Why, even if I wanted to, those giants over in Lewistown would eat up a little guy like you for breakfast."

I pictured the mighty eighth-graders of Lewistown grinding my puny bones between their molars, and I almost laughed. Then I decided it wasn't so funny.

In fact, the whole thing was starting to seem pretty tragic.

I went back to the shrimp squad and spent the rest of the period sitting in the bleachers while Coach Simpson worked with his players. Boyd Pearson was chosen to play center. He was heavy on his feet, and his free throws weren't the greatest, but there was no denying it: Boyd the Bully was a giant.

Right then I would have given him every tuna fish

sandwich in the world for four more inches in height.

I was depressed when I left the gym. The thought of going to the games and having to cheer for Boyd Pearson made me want to puke. I knew it was disloyal—be true to your school, and all that. But deep down I hoped Boyd would turn out to be the worst center in the history of Wheaton, Pennsylvania. I hoped that the giants of Lewistown would eat him for breakfast, lunch, and dinner, with maybe a Boyd Pearson snack thrown in for good measure. I hoped—

"Hi, Kyle."

Right then I forgot about the shrimp squad, and not shooting up, and the red, sneering face of Boyd the Bully. I turned and smiled at Celia Simkewicz.

"Great to be back, huh?" She pointed at the shiny hallway and made a face.

While I tried to think up a witty answer, I checked out Celia's appearance. Short, upturned nose. Shoulder-length blond hair (real blond, not the dull yellow kind, like mine). Teeth the tiniest bit crooked in front.

Gazing at Celia's crooked teeth, a weird feeling of happiness came over me, like when you get home from a long trip and your house is still there, and your room, and all your stuff is right where you left it.

"Back?" I said blankly.

Celia paused. "Back in school. Here," she explained, pointing at the linoleum floor.

"Oh. Right." Here, stupid. The happy feeling vanished

as the blood rushed to my face. "Yeah, it's great. Really great." I saw Kim and Gwendolyn, Celia's pals, creep into view. Their hands were cupped over their mouths and they were doing goofy things with their eyes while they watched me fumble the social ball on the free throw line.

"Well, got to get going," I told her. Then I shot through the nearest door, before their giggles reached my ears.

Too late. Rowena said that girls laughed at people they liked, but I knew the depressing truth: I was no better at talking to Celia Simkewicz than I was at making basketball teams. Maybe Coach Simpson was right about his thyroid theory. Something was definitely out of whack.

"Hi there," a voice called.

I jumped. Then I realized I was in a classroom, and someone was sitting at the desk up front. It was Ms. Loomis, my English teacher from last year.

She smiled. "I didn't mean to startle you, Kyle. I thought you were here for the meeting."

"Meeting?"

"For the Knowledge Bowl. It was posted on the activities board this morning. I was starting to wonder if anyone saw it." She checked her watch. "Well, I'll give them a few more minutes. You're welcome to stay. In fact, I hope you'll sign up for the team, Kyle. You'd be a great addition."

I was about to tell her that making teams wasn't my specialty, but she looked so pleased to see me, I didn't have the heart. Ms. Loomis was just about my favorite teacher. She was younger than most of the teachers, and she really cared about teaching and about the kids in her class. Ms. Loomis got so excited about books, she made you want to read them too, even though you didn't always understand what she saw in them. Or in some of her students, for that matter.

I took a seat. "Just one question," I said, while Ms. Loomis erased the blackboard. "What's a Knowledge Bowl?"

She laughed. "So much for posting announcements! Well, as long as you're here, I'll tell you. It's a student knowledge tournament held every January in the state capital. Four kids are picked from each school to answer questions on different subjects. The schools with the highest scores send teams to the semi-finals, and then the top two teams play for the big prize. This year it's a computer system for the winning school."

"Does the second runner-up get a lovely dining room set and a year's supply of dill pickles?"

Ms. Loomis tried to look stern. "This is no joke, Kyle. The kids who win will have to know a great deal about math and history and literature and current events. And I intend to come up with the best team ever."

"Great," I said. "When do we start?"

"Not until we get a few more volunteers. But before anybody goes to Harrisburg, our team has to qualify. And that means passing a pretty hard test. Or rather, a couple of them. Think you can do it?"

I looked at Ms. Loomis. I knew what Dad would say if he were sitting here: To beat the competition, you have to be the best. You have to *believe* you're the best.

I wasn't sure if I did. So far, today wasn't exactly championship material. I didn't make the basketball team, again. Boyd Pearson called me a shrimp. Coach Simpson thought I needed a thyroid transplant. And Celia and her friends had nearly split their guts over my great social skills.

Not a real confidence booster, any way you looked at it.

Then I saw something out of the corner of my eye. It was Rowena Whipple, marching through the door, a determined look on her freckled face.

"Let's do it," I said quietly. "Let's go for the gold."

CHAPTER 4

When I got home from school, Mom was out on the patio. She had her paints and easel set up, and she was staring fiercely at a flower arrangement on the picnic table.

"Be with you in a sec," she said without turning around. "I just want to get this picture set in my mind."

I dropped my books on a chair and waited while she studied the flowers. Finally she put down her brush. "I knew primroses were a bad idea," she muttered. "Too much detail for watercolor."

I came over and looked at the sheet of heavy paper tacked to the easel. A rough outline of the flowers was already sketched in pencil. "Are you going to enter the Village Art Show again?"

She smiled and began packing up her paints. "Maybe," she said. "But this isn't for the show. You know Mary Ellen Baker, Susie's mom?"

I nodded. Susie Baker was in Brian's class at Wheaton High.

"She's started a small greeting card company. There

was a notice about it down at the Neighborhood Guild. Anyway, I showed her some of my work, and she thought I could do a good job with her line of floral cards. So now I'm trying to learn how to paint still lifes for fun and profit."

"Are you getting paid for this, Mom?"

She unpinned the sketch paper and rolled it up. "That's the idea. It won't be a vast fortune, but it's a start. Who knows, this may be the beginning of a whole new career. Today, Sunshine Greeting Cards, tomorrow—well, more greeting cards!"

I laughed. Mom did too.

Then she added, "Listen, Kyle, don't say anything about this to your dad. Just until—you know—I've got something to show for my labors. Okay?"

"Sure, Mom." I nodded. "Mum's the word."

"Mums . . . chrysanthemums? Not a bad idea. Why didn't I think of that? They'd be perfect for watercolors!" And she hugged me.

But as I helped carry her easel into the house, I felt a little creepy. Another secret. The old code of silence, one more time.

But I didn't say anything. Mom was happy about her new painting project. If she didn't want Dad to know, it was none of my business.

Around six o'clock Brian came charging through the front door. "What's for dinner? I'm so hungry I could eat a horse. Saddle and all."

"Where have you been?" Mom called from the kitchen where we were making a salad. Meaning I cut up the carrots, and Mom did everything else. "I was starting to worry. Kyle's been home for hours."

"Practice." Bri was panting and his face dripped with sweat. "School's started, remember?"

Mom frowned. "Brian, no matter what your coach thinks, there's more to school than basketball. I don't want your practice cutting into study time, okay?"

"Right, Sarge." He grinned and saluted. "So, how about some chow? A steak, medium-rare? Maybe a couple of baked potatoes? Lemon meringue pie?"

"Sorry, kid. I thought I'd thaw out a casserole. Or I could warm up one of those deluxe pizzas from the supermarket. The ones with all the pepperoni and sausage on top?"

Brian didn't look thrilled at the idea of pizza for dinner, but he just shrugged. "Where's Dad?"

I glanced at Mom. She was opening the freezer and taking out the pizza. "Working late, I guess. You heard what he said—he's going to be putting in some long hours for a while. Until the crunch at the office is over."

She went over to preheat the oven. "Look, why don't you guys get ready for dinner. I'm sure Dad will be along soon."

Brian shrugged again and headed for the stairs. But before he reached them, he looked across the room and caught my eye.

I knew what that glance meant, but I didn't want to think about it. I turned back to cutting up the carrots, while I listened to Bri's sneakers squeak up the stairs.

Maybe Dad really did have extra work at the office. Maybe there was nothing to worry about. Still, we both knew what usually happened when Dad was late.

It meant he'd been drinking.

I was ten years old when I figured that out. Up until then, I'd always looked up to my dad; I thought he was the greatest guy in the world. He was never too busy to help with homework, or take you to a ballgame, or comfort you when you were scared or mad about something. If I did everything right, I figured, someday I'd grow up to be just like Dad.

And then a weird thing started happening. Every few months, instead of my real dad, this other guy would show up. The Stranger.

It began with him coming home late for dinner. I didn't know anything about drinking then. All I knew was that Dad's face didn't look right, and the words that came out of his mouth didn't sound right. And all of a sudden nothing Brian or I did was right. The Stranger would sit down at the table and start talking in a real loud voice. He'd get mad about stuff—little stuff, stupid stuff. Like if someone reached past him for the butter, or you ate your peas with a spoon, stuff like that.

And then he'd get mean. And he'd yell. After a while Brian started yelling back. But I never said a word. I'd just sneak up to my room and cry. And hope with all my heart that the mean, loud Stranger would go away and leave us alone. And let my real dad come home.

Sure enough, by the next day the Stranger was gone.

But sooner or later he always came back. And the same thing would happen all over again.

I knew Mom was worried. She never talked about it, but I could tell by the way she watched Dad when he came home, to see what kind of mood he was in. Or like tonight, when she'd start dinner without him. That way, Brian and I would be done eating by the time he got in, and Dad couldn't pick a fight with anybody. Especially Brian.

It wasn't like the Stranger showed up every night. But sometimes I wished he'd just move in for good. Then maybe I could get used to the way things were, and forget about them.

Instead, a crummy feeling of suspense hovered over our house, over all of us. I hated that feeling. A week or a month would go by, and Dad would seem like his old self, and I'd start to relax and think, maybe it's finally over.

But it never was. Not really.

And lately it was getting worse. I could see it in Mom's watchful eyes, and in the angry way Brian slammed around the house. I tried to think of something to do. Maybe if I just told him, "Dad, you're making everybody crazy and unhappy. There's this place I saw in the phone book, this hospital where you could go . . ."

Dad would nod and say something like, "I had no idea I was hurting you guys. You're right, Kyle. It's time I got a handle on this drinking thing once and for all." Then everything would get back to normal, and Mom and Brian would say, "Wow, Kyle, whatever you said to Dad, it really worked." And I'd just smile and feel like a hero.

Deep down, though, I knew I'd never say anything like that. Besides, Dad would just pretend I was making the whole thing up. Because that was the worst part of all: Dad had turned into a liar.

I was sure that he knew about the Stranger too, but he'd never admit it. He just made up these crummy excuses for him. Whenever he overslept, and woke up late and groggy, I'd hear him on the phone to his supervisor: "Sorry I missed the meeting, Jack. Guess I got one of those twenty-four-hour bugs. Kids must have brought it home from school." But no one in the house was sick, except for him.

Or the time he ruined Mom's birthday by showing up late and starting a big argument. The next day the whole house was filled with bouquets from the florist's shop. "I'm just an old bear," he told her, and you could tell he meant it, that he really was sorry.

All the same, as I headed upstairs to wash my hands, I sure hoped Dad was only working late tonight.

"More salad?"

I shook my head. Then I polished off the last slice of pepperoni pizza and wiped my mouth. "Guess what? My teacher, Ms. Loomis, wants me to try out for the Knowledge Bowl team."

Brian grinned. "No kidding, Squirt? You going to Harrisburg for the annual Brain Drain?"

"What's the Brain Drain?" Mom smiled expectantly. "Something good, I hope."

"It's this contest they hold in the state capital every year," Brian explained. "Some teachers' group sponsors it. The schools send these teams and they try to answer questions about math and history."

"And English and social studies," I added. "If it's mostly math, I won't have a prayer."

"Hey, I know!" Brian snapped his fingers. "You could get one of those tiny calculators and hide it in your belt buckle. Bingo! Instant math whiz." He chuckled at the thought.

Mom looked at him and frowned. "That isn't funny, Brian. Cheating isn't a joking matter, not in this house."

She got up to clear the table. "Now, don't you worry, Kyle. We'll all be very proud if you make the team."

"Except for Dad," Brian put in. "Don't expect him to get too excited, unless they make you captain of the whole team. *And* you cream everybody else in the state. *And* you win an all-expenses paid scholarship to the college of your choice—"

Mom yanked Brian's empty salad bowl off the table. "Brian Maxwell, I'm going to pretend I didn't hear a word of that. In fact, we're all going to pretend you didn't say it."

"Why not?" Brian mumbled. "It's true, isn't it? Nothing's ever good enough for Dad." He got up from the table and headed for the front door. "That's a hot one, if you ask me. Nothing's ever good enough, when *he*'s the one who—"

I held my breath. Mom looked tense and angry, like she didn't want to hear it either. But Bri had already scooped up his basketball from the corner. A second later, we heard him out in the driveway shooting imaginary three-pointers.

Without a word I helped Mom clear the table. When the dishwasher was loaded, she gazed down at me and then tapped me on the nose. "Don't listen to Brian. He's just angry at the world. You know, teenage stuff."

"Sure, Mom," I said.

She smiled. "And if you need help with math for that tournament, your dad's the one to ask. He knows that stuff inside and out. You have to, to earn a business degree, right?"

"Right," I said.

That's when I heard it: the slam of a car door. I waited for the murmur of voices, as Dad greeted Brian. A minute later, he came through the door and plopped his heavy sample case down on the hall table.

"In here," Mom called. I focused on wiping up the counter next to the sink. Neither of us looked at each other.

"Whew." Dad appeared in the doorway. His shirt was rumpled, his tie undone, and his face was tired. But it wasn't red, and his eyes looked clear. For the first time since I got home from school, I began to relax.

"Tough day, honey?" Mom asked. She went over and gave him a kiss.

"Endless," he groaned. "That new guy, Hicks, is a real backbreaker. But he'll get results. You wait and see."

He went over to the refrigerator and took out a can of beer. Closing his eyes, he held the frosty can against his forehead. When he looked up, he saw me watching him from the corner of the room.

"Hey there, champ!" he called. "How's it feel to be an eighth-grader?"

I shrugged. "It's okay." I felt Mom's eyes on me, nudging me to go on, so I added, "My teacher thinks I could be on the Knowledge Bowl team this year. It's—it's sort of an honor, I guess."

I waited for Dad to say something. Please don't ask about basketball, I thought. Just don't even bring it up. Let this be enough.

Maybe it was the "honor" bit. But Dad's face kind of lit up, and he came over and threw a few shadow punches at me, which is what my dad does when he's pleased about something.

"Way to go, Kyle," he kept saying. "That's my kid."

He stood back and beamed at me. "Hey, way to go," he repeated.

It didn't seem like a good time to ask for help with math. Not with Mom beaming at me too. So I just smiled and nodded, until Dad cracked open his beer and Mom went over to rescue his dinner from the oven, and I could escape to Rowena's.

CHAPTER 5

Arnold "the Rat" Whipple was guarding the front door when I reached Rowena's house. There was a disgusting orange ring around the Rat's mouth, incriminating evidence that the Whipples were having Spaghetti-Os for dinner, and his hands looked like twin hunks of used flypaper. Arnold "the Rat" was eternally sticky. Everything he touched stuck to him like he was magnetized.

In a word, Arnold was repulsive. His nose ran like a faucet, his hair was caked with jam and chocolate syrup, and he drooled when he stared at you. Arnold "the Rat" Whipple made Dennis the Menace look like Goldilocks. I loathed him.

I know some people think all kids are adorable and that you'd have to be a real creep to hate a five-year-old. Those people never met the Rat. Besides, what went on between me and Arnold had nothing to do with age. It didn't matter if he was five or fifty: This was war.

Just in case I felt guilty about it, the Rat made sure I knew the feeling was mutual. He brought out the worst in me. He made me feel like Boyd Pearson, he really did. I couldn't wait until Arnold got out of kindergarten so I could steal his lunch.

We got things off on a friendly note right away. Arnold squinted up his eyes and showed me his horrible orange tongue. Then he thrust out his stomach so that it looked like he'd swallowed a watermelon. "You're a booger!" he informed me.

"Hi, Arnold," I said, like I was greeting an old pal. I knew it drove him nuts when I was nice to him. "Is your sister around?"

"Which one, booger?"

"You know which one. Rowena. You want to let me in, so I can say hi?"

"Nope." And then, just in case I thought I was welcome, the Rat spit on me.

I looked around to see if anyone was watching. Then I made a grab for his fat little stomach. "C'mere, you little creep, try that again if you're so smart," I hissed, while the Rat tried to kick his way out of my grasp.

"Mommeee!" he wailed.

Talk about fighting dirty. In an instant Mrs. Whipple was at the door, a dish towel in her hands. I let go of the Rat, and he went scooting behind the Mommy battlements.

"Hello, Kyle," she said. "Was Arnold being naughty again?" She smiled and ruffled his sticky hair.

Would you call a terrorist naughty? Then again, even terrorists must have mothers.

I wiped off my pants. "No, just a little friendly spitting

contest," I answered, while Arnold stuck out his tongue at me. "Is Rowena done eating?"

Mrs. Whipple didn't seem sure. She always looked a little dazed, which is maybe what having six kids does to a person. Just trying to keep track of all the Whipples' names was enough to stump most people. There was Rebecca, Soren, Roxanne, Friedrich, Rowena, and Arnold. All the boys were named after dead philosophers; the girls' names came from characters in books Mrs. Whipple liked.

The girls' names also all started with the letter R, which was very confusing. "She could have named you after the characters in *Little Women*," I complained to Rowena once. "Those were pretty good names, weren't they? Besides, they were all different."

"But there were four of them," Rowena said. "At that rate, Arnold would have ended up as Beth."

Which would have served him right, if you ask me.

No, if I were going to have six kids, I would name them after *The Brady Bunch*. Or Mrs. Whipple could have gone with a *Snow White* theme. That way, she'd even have a name left over, in case she felt like having another kid.

Sneezy Whipple. Now there's a great name.

I followed Mrs. Whipple and Arnold into the house. It was a big, messy, noisy place, and I liked it a lot. All the Whipples and their friends were always hanging around, except for Mr. Whipple. He was a commuter airline pilot, which meant he was usually 15,000 feet above Pittsburgh. The friendly skies must seem pretty peaceful after a few days at home.

There were also a couple Whipple dogs, a million Whipple cats, and some very brave Whipple pigeons who lived in the backyard. Any day now I expected to see a pig moseying through the kitchen.

Instead I found Rowena sitting at the table, making little designs in her plate of Spaghetti-Os. I sat down next to her and waved goodbye to the Rat, who was being led off for his bath.

He made a terrible face. "Booger!"

I shrugged. "Yeah, well, I guess boogers don't have to take baths if they don't feel like it. Right, buddy?"

Arnold looked crestfallen. I could hear his screams of rage as Mrs. Whipple hauled him up the stairs.

"He's in his booger phase," Rowena commented. She reached past me and grabbed a piece of bread off a big pile in the middle of the table.

"What's a booger phase?" I asked.

Rowena was gouging holes in the piece of bread and popping them in her mouth. "Naughty words," she explained. "Go up to him and say 'poo-poo' some time. He practically has convulsions."

That sounded promising. Then again, judging from the noise overhead, the convulsions had already started. We listened to Arnold empty the bathtub while Rowena finished her dinner. Then she got up, dumped her plate in the sink, and headed out to the backyard.

As soon as we got outside, she gave me a long look. "Well?"

"Well what? Well, did I make the basketball team? Negativo. Did a bunch of weird girls giggle and make goo-goo eyes at me? Absolutely. Am I thrilled about it? Not exactly."

Rowena rolled her eyes. "Oh, Ky-uhl," she said. "I meant the Knowledge Bowl team. Do you think you want to do it?"

I thought back to the meeting I'd crashed. After Rowena showed up, some more kids straggled in until there were about ten of us. Then Ms. Loomis told everybody about the tournament—how we'd have to pass a bunch of tests, and practice after school, and then compete with the other schools in the county in order to get to the state capital. She made it sound harder than winning the Tournament of Champions on *Jeopardy*.

"I don't know," I said, as honestly as I could. "Sounds like a lot of work."

"I think it sounds like fun," Rowena said. "Besides, Ms. Loomis really wants you to do it."

"She does?"

Rowena nodded. "Anyway, Kyle," she said, kneeling down to poke her finger through the mesh of the pigeon cage, "don't you want this year to mean something? I mean, you're always moaning about that stupid basketball team. Big deal! Anyone can play basketball as long as they've got the right kind of stork legs."

I pictured Boyd Pearson. Stork legs didn't come close. Try redwoods.

Her brown eyes sparkled earnestly. "This way, you

could prove that brain is better than brawn. Besides," she said, "if we did it together, we could help each other."

"How?" I handed Fenwick, a well-fed gray and white pigeon, a piece of corn. He swallowed it in one dignified peck.

"You've got all that history and modern authors stuff down cold. I'm better at math and science. So—we could study for the tests together. Once we make the team, we can just split up the questions we're good at."

"Sounds like a snap," I said. I still wasn't sure I wanted to do it. Ms. Loomis or no Ms. Loomis, Dad or no Dad, I didn't have anything to prove. My life was tough enough without taking on every kid in Central County.

Then I looked at Rowena. Her face was scrunched up just like old Arnold's. "Okay, answer me this," I said. "Say I decide to knock myself out, and we study together, and take all these tests. What's in it for me?"

Rowena's eyes were tiny little slits by now. "What's in it for you? Boy, that's a wonderful attitude, Kyle. What's the matter with you? Does everything have to come with a guaranteed gold medal attached?"

She scrambled to her feet, startling Fenwick, who whirred to the opposite end of the cage. "You can't do anything unless you get to be the big attraction, can you? Like that dumb basketball team! Every year you let Coach Simpson talk you out of playing. I mean, if you really *liked* playing basketball, you'd make him give you a chance. But no, just because you're not King Brian the Second, or a thousand feet tall like that creep Boyd, you give up.

Well, fine. But don't expect me to cheer about it!"

Rowena hurtled off toward the house. I got to my feet and ran after her. I was starting to catch on. Rowena wanted to go for the Knowledge Bowl. And she wanted me to do it with her.

Let's face it: She needed me. And if I was going to get anywhere, I needed her too.

When I caught up with her, I grabbed her arm. I didn't want to admit she was right about the basketball team, but she'd hit it on the nose. And it stung.

The truth was, I wasn't crazy about basketball. But when you're a Maxwell, you don't have much choice. I'd been tossing balls at the hoop over our garage ever since I could remember, and mostly missing. I could still hear Dad yelling in my ear, "C'mon, champ. One more try. You can do it if you really want to. Let's go!"

I wasn't so sure about all that other stuff—it wasn't like I had to win a gold medal; I just wanted to be invisible. It beat being a failure any day.

Anyway, that's what I told Rowena. "Look," I said, "I don't care what's in it for me, all right? I don't even have to be on the team. I could help you study, if you want. History's just a bunch of dates. You'd catch on fast. Either way, it's up to you. Okay? Okay, Rowe?"

Rowena paused, one long, skinny leg braced against the back steps. Then she gave me one of her withering looks. "Oh, Kyle," she sighed. "You can be such a jerk sometimes."

But I could tell she'd forgiven me. It made me want to

give her something in return. I mean, when you're a jerk, guilt comes with the territory.

So I did. I gave her one of my secrets.

"What do you know about Celia Simkewicz?" I asked. That's all I had to say. Rowena plopped down on the steps, and a slow mischievous grin stretched across her face.

"Celia Simkewicz, huh?" she said. "Well, answer me this. What's in it for me if I tell you?"

I sighed. "The Knowledge Bowl." Rowena's grin widened. "We go all the way to the state capital," I said. "Winner takes all."

CHAPTER 6

Here's what Rowena knew about Celia:

1. Celia Simkewicz really was nice. It wasn't just an act.

"Gee," I said sarcastically, "that's a relief."

"No, there's a difference," Rowena insisted. "Certain people—well, I won't mention names—but certain people pretend they're glad to see you or that they like your outfit, but they don't mean it, they just want to be popular. Celia isn't like that. She's sincere."

I tried to picture Boyd Pearson pretending that he liked my shirt when he really wanted to rip my face off. That would never happen in a million years. Girls 101. It was pretty interesting.

2. Celia was an only child.

"An only child?" I said. "You mean she doesn't have twelve sisters with names that begin with the letter C?"

Score: one withering stare. I decided to shut up and listen.

3. The Simkewiczes lived in the north end of Wheaton. We lived in the south end. The north end houses were

newer, with little shingled roofs, and tiny lawns with tiny trees out front. Mom sold a lot of townhouses there.

The south end was the original part of Wheaton; the houses were bigger and older, a little shabby, maybe, but more permanent looking. I felt sort of sorry for Celia, staring out at her itty-bitty front yard every day.

Our school was also in the south end. That meant Celia had to take the bus. This was bad news; the only time I could talk to her was during school.

I caught myself. Talk to her? That was a good one. Whenever Celia tried to talk to me, I turned into a tongue-tied moron. What difference did it make *where* she lived?

"Listen," I said, trying to sound casual, "you're a girl, Rowena. What do girls like to talk about? Just in general, of course."

"You mean with boys? Or with each other?"

"Well—let's say with boys. With me, for instance."

She burst out laughing. "Kyle, what's the big deal? If you want to talk to Celia, just walk up to her and ask how her classes are going. Tell her something funny that happened to you. Make her laugh."

"I don't seem to have any problem making girls laugh," I said. "In fact, that's my specialty. They see me coming and practically have hysterics."

"Well, tell her something sad, then. Something personal. You don't have to do a comedy routine. Just be yourself. Girls aren't creatures from another planet, you know."

"They aren't?" I was kidding—sort of.

"Of course not. After all, I'm a girl, and you're not scared to talk to me."

"Well, I'm not scared to talk to Celia Simkewicz either!"

Rowena grinned. "Then prove it," she said.

I waited until lunch. Celia and her friends were sitting up near the stage—the cafeteria doubled as an auditorium—and I could tell they were done eating.

I paid a quick visit to the boys' room, just to gather my thoughts. Back in the lunchroom, I started to walk, saunter, actually, over to the table. Then I saw there were five of them, counting Celia. Too many girls to face alone. This called for backup.

I grabbed Scott Kenyon, who was heading for the door.

"Come on," I said. "I want to ask Celia something."

He looked at my hand, which was wrapped around his arm. "So? You need a bodyguard?"

"More or less," I said, hustling him off toward the stage.

As we approached ground zero, I tried to think of something to say. The girls' heads were clumped together, and they were whispering. My heart began to pound. Right then, I would rather have faced a hungry grizzly bear, or even Boyd Pearson, than a clump of whispering girls.

Scott seemed to understand. He casually punched me on the arm. I nodded brusquely. Two buddies, facing the dangers of the unknown. Butch Cassidy and Sundance. Kirk and Spock. The Lone Ranger and Tonto.

I nudged Scott in the ribs. We were almost at the table.

Suddenly the whispering stopped. Celia looked up and saw us. "Hi, Kyle," she said, and smiled.

My brain froze. My throat turned to sandpaper. "Hi," I croaked.

A spasm of giggles erupted from the assembled girls. It was like standing in a hail of machine gun bullets. Scott ducked behind me.

What were they laughing at? I licked my lips and tried to ignore the giggle barrage. "So," I said, "great to be back, huh?"

Celia nodded. I wished she'd say something, so that I could answer, but she seemed to be waiting for me to go on. I took a deep breath. "Ms. Loomis was telling me about this Knowledge Bowl thing. Thought I might try out. Have you heard about it?"

This was the most I had ever said to Celia Simkewicz. A speech, practically. I could feel Scott shuffling behind me. The girls were poised, waiting for more comic relief.

Celia's forehead puckered. "Knowledge Bowl?"

Huge pools of sweat were gathering under my shirt. "Yeah, you have to answer questions about different stuff. All the schools compete for a prize." I shrugged. "I don't know. I thought it might be kind of fun."

Celia laughed, but it wasn't a mean laugh. "You have to be pretty brainy for something like that. I don't think my grades are good enough. The classes seem a lot harder this year, don't you think?"

"Did you see that reading list for science?" Kim, one of

the loudest gigglers, asked. "If he tests us on that, I just know I'm going to flunk!"

There was a grumble of agreement about the reading list. I began to relax. At least they weren't staring at me.

"Like, what's the use of studying?" another girl, Marcy, said. "Half the time, they're just trying to trick you into looking dumb."

"What do you mean?" I asked. "The teachers are trying to trick you? Why would they do that?"

She ignored me. "My brother—he's a sophomore now—he says the only way to make it fair is to cheat." She looked around the table. "Well, not cheat, exactly, but you know. Even things up."

There was silence.

Then Scott cleared his throat. "How?" he asked. "How does your brother even things up?"

Marcy's eyes glittered. "He tells them he's sick. On the day of the test. So then he has to take a make-up test, but by then one of the other kids has given him the answers."

"What if it's a different test?" I asked.

"But it's not," Marcy insisted. "Or else, if he tells them he's *really* sick, sometimes they'll give him a take-home exam. So my dad can help him."

"My dad would never help me," Kim announced. "Half the time he won't even look over my homework. My mom either," she added.

"I heard about this kid who was a computer whiz," Scott put in. I noticed he'd sidled up next to me. "He found out that the teachers kept all the tests on the school's computer system. Except it had a password. So one day when he was in the computer lab he entered the teachers' names—backwards. Sure enough, there were all the tests, for the whole year!"

Even Marcy looked impressed at that.

"So all he had to do was look up the answers, see?" Scott finished.

"I could never do anything like that," Celia said. Then she sighed. "I'm just terrible with computers. No matter what I do, I can't get them to work right."

"So what's wrong with studying?" I asked. "I mean, in the time it would take to crack a computer code, you could have studied for the test. Right?"

Silence. Everybody was staring at me, including Scott. He looked kind of mad, like I'd ruined his story.

"But that's not the point," Kim said. "It's the teachers— it's like they don't want you to get a good grade. I mean, I study all the time and it doesn't do me any good. Besides," she said, "you know how parents are if you don't get A's." She made a face.

"Mine get real mad," one girl said. "My father even tried to bribe me. He said he'd pay me five dollars for every A on my report card. So far it hasn't worked."

Everyone around the table tried to figure how much money they'd make getting A's. I was glad when the bell rang. I watched Celia gather up her books.

"Listen," I said quickly, "Ms. Loomis doesn't care if you're a brain or not. Why don't you come to our next meeting? It's on Wednesday, after school."

She looked at me shyly. "It's nice of you to invite me. But I haven't decided what after-school activities I'm going to do yet. My friends are all trying out for cheer-leading."

I glanced back at the table. I noticed Scott had hung around and was talking to a couple of the girls.

"Well, just thought I'd pass it along," I told Celia. "You know, the more the merrier."

She nodded, and I found myself staring at her silky, golden hair, the same color as Cindy the dog's coat. In fact, I found myself wanting to touch it. Not even because I liked Celia, which I did. Just because it was so pretty.

"Hey, Maxwell. Haven't seen you at practice this week. What's the matter? Did Coach Simpson raise the yardstick on you again?"

I looked up. Boyd Pearson's big red mouth was hanging open, as usual, and there was a sprig of parsley stuck between his teeth. Boyd must be the only human on earth who thought you were supposed to actually eat parsley, but I wasn't in the mood to point this out.

He clapped a huge paw on my shoulder. "Gee," he said, "the season just won't be the same without you, Maxwell. *Again.*"

He gave Celia a meaningful smile. To my relief, she didn't smile back.

And then, just when I figured I was out of the woods, Boyd struck a fatal blow.

"Oh, and Maxwell? I hate to tell you this, buddy, but the barn door's open." He gave a hearty guffaw.

"Wouldn't want you to catch pneumonia or anything. Know what I mean?"

With another bone-shuddering clap on the back, Boyd moved off. Celia looked confused for a moment, and then embarrassed. And then she giggled.

A second later, I realized what she was laughing at. What they were *all* laughing at.

My fly was open.

CHAPTER 7

It must be written somewhere in stone. Just when life starts looking up, the old roller coaster hits a curve, and the next thing you know, your stomach's somewhere near your brain, and the ground's zooming up at you.

That's how I felt after the zipper fiasco. Like no matter what I did, I couldn't get a break.

And then Wednesday came. The pits. I knew it the minute I walked into the house: The Stranger was back.

I'd stayed after school to help plan our strategy for the Knowledge Bowl. Ms. Loomis drew a big chart with the ten members of the team listed on it. Only four kids could compete, but everyone had a shot at making it to the county tryouts.

Next, we worked on subject areas. Rowena was the clear champ at math, and everybody said I'd do great on the literature section. "Good," I said. "That means I can skip the math test, right?"

Ms. Loomis smiled. "Sorry, Kyle. It doesn't work that way. The rules state that unless every member of the final team passes all the subject tests, they can't represent the school."

"Don't worry, Kyle," Rowena said. "I'll drill you until you've got holes in your head!"

The teacher beamed. "Teamwork's the key," she said. "And that goes for the rest of you, too. From now until we take the tests next month, I want you to split up into study teams. Next time we meet I'll have sample tests you guys can review for practice."

I left the meeting wondering how I could cram Rowena's head full of twentieth-century authors in one month. Maybe I could make a cassette that Rowena could play under her pillow at night. "Ernest Hemingway wrote *A Farewell to Arms, The Sun Also Rises, The Old Man and the Sea . . .*"

Just as I got to *For Whom the Bell Tolls,* I heard a buzzer sound. I paused at the gym door. The basketball team was holding its first after-school practice.

There they were, the Wheaton Warriors, whooping it up on the court. I watched Boyd crash up and down a few times. He looked like a baby elephant stampeding through a watering hole. For all his height, he wasn't too hot at sinking shots. Besides, he threw so many elbows, none of the other players wanted to get near him.

At the other end of the gym the cheering squad was holding its own practice. I spotted Kim and Marcy jumping up and down, waving their pom-poms. Then a blond head popped up. It was Celia, wearing the white sweater and blue skirt of a Wheaton cheerleader. She looked beautiful. Beautiful, and totally out of reach.

I dug my hands in my pockets and edged out the door.

Celia had picked her after-school activity, all right. And it didn't include me.

Not that I could blame her. What did I have to offer? Short, tongue-tied, and I couldn't keep my zipper closed. Some hero. Still, the thought of Celia and Boyd Pearson under the same roof for the whole season made my skin crawl.

All the way home, I tried to pretend I was getting taller. "Guess what," I'd tell Coach Simpson. "It's finally happening—I'm starting to shoot up!"

"Great news, son," he'd answer. "You know, the Pearson kid just isn't working out like I hoped. How'd you like to start against the Lewistown Giants next Friday?"

But when I rolled in the door, I didn't feel one inch taller. Then I noticed Dad's briefcase was lying on the couch. A stack of papers was spread out on the coffee table, next to a glass of melting ice.

I went to the kitchen to grab a snack. There was a note from Mom on the refrigerator, telling me to take some chops out of the freezer. I took them out, and was reaching in the cookie jar for a brownie, when Dad walked into the kitchen.

He frowned when he saw me. "Oh. I thought it was your mother."

I watched him take out the ice cube tray. "Didn't you see the note?" I asked. "She must be at that open house tonight. For those new condos going up in the north end."

"What note?"

I held it out to him. Dad looked at it for a second. Then he crumpled it and tossed it on the counter. "Great," he said. "What does a guy have to do to get some dinner around here?"

I bit into the brownie and chewed slowly. Dad was moving around the kitchen muttering to himself. I reached for another brownie, figuring I'd take it up to my room, when he turned and barked, "Where's your brother? He out selling condos too?"

My fingers closed around the brownie. "Brian? He must still be at practice. He usually doesn't get in until six."

The Stranger narrowed his eyes. As he studied me, my heart sank down into my toes. Here we go, a little voice whispered. Here we go again.

"Six, huh?" He gazed at me for another moment. "So what are you doing home?"

I considered asking him the same thing. Instead I settled for a shrug.

He was looking through the cupboards, banging the cabinet doors. I gauged the distance from the cookie jar to the door. Thirty seconds, tops.

Too late. He'd found what he was looking for. I heard him take down the bottle and unscrew the cap. A clatter of ice cubes hit the glass. Clink, clank. "I asked you a question," the Stranger said, as he poured himself a drink.

"You did?"

"You just said your brother was at practice. Don't you have practice?" Dad leaned against the counter and took a sip of his drink.

"You mean for the Knowledge Bowl? It just got out." I put the brownie back in the jar, and began edging for the door.

"I meant the team. You know, organized sports? Basketball?" The ice in the glass rattled as Dad set it down. He was silent for a moment. When he spoke again, he sounded mad. "Don't tell me you got scrubbed again?"

"Well, I—"

"Tell me the truth, Kyle. Did you or didn't you?"

"The coach says I'm too short, Dad. But listen, remember how I told you about this knowledge tournament thing? How it's like an honor and stuff? I think I have a real shot at that." I heard my voice babbling away. But it was kind of pointless. Talking to Dad when he was drinking was your basic lose-lose situation.

The Stranger shook his head. "I can't believe this! I've got one kid who's All-State in everything he ever tried out for. And then I've got you." He sighed and picked up his glass. "What am I supposed to do with you, Kyle?" he asked. "Pretend I'm happy about this?"

"No, Dad, it's just that Coach Simpson says—"

"I don't want to hear any more about the coach. I don't buy that junk, okay?" His voice rose, a loud, thick blur. "This is about competitiveness, that's what this is about. Showing people you've got what it takes!"

He started talking about how I was this big disappointment to him, this big failure, how everything I did reflected on him. His voice got louder. "When I was your age, I didn't let some loser coach tell me what to do. I had what it took! But you . . . ." He glared at me. "You won't even give it your best shot. My own son—a screw-up!"

I tried to imagine I was stuck in a room with a loud radio playing terrible music. Or sitting in the dentist's chair while they revved up the drill. You know sooner or later it's going to stop. But that doesn't make you want to sit back and relax.

What I wanted to do was cover my ears, but that would only make things worse. So I tried not to listen. But it was tough.

I wasn't sure how long I stood there, tuning Dad out, when the front door slammed and Brian walked into the kitchen.

He looked at Dad and then at me. "Where's Mom?" he asked.

"Your mother?" Dad gazed at Bri for a moment. Then he shrugged. "Your mother is a working woman," Dad explained. "She's abandoned us."

Brian frowned. He crossed the room and peered into my face. "Don't you have some homework to do?" he said. In an undertone, he added, "I'll take care of this. You okay?"

I nodded.

"Good. Then beat it."

He didn't have to tell me twice. I shot a look at Dad. He seemed distracted, like he wasn't really focusing on me anymore. When he turned to get some more ice, I scooted out of the kitchen and up the stairs.

I lay on my bed and stared at the ceiling. Scraps of loud

words filtered up from below. I heard Brian yell, "Why don't you just lay off him?" and then Dad's hot reply. Even though I hadn't done anything to make him mad, a crazy tidal wave of guilt crashed over me, and I thought, "He's right, it's all my fault. If only I'd made the basketball team, Dad would have been proud of me, and then he wouldn't have to drink so much." If only I wasn't such a screw-up.

I rolled onto my stomach and shoved my face in the pillow. That was the part that hurt the most: feeling like I'd let him down. Stranger or no Stranger, he was still my dad. And dads were supposed to be proud of their kids. Weren't they?

When Mom came home, I was propped up on my bed, staring at some math problems. So far, they didn't make any sense. Maybe Rowena could explain to me why $x + y = z$ some of the time, but other times they don't.

Math drove me crazy. I hate things that look so logical, but really aren't. Now, a poem is always a poem. You can read things into it if you want, but every time you open the book, the same words are there. You can do whatever you want with them. There aren't all these crummy rules. When you're a screw-up, the last thing you need is more rules.

There was a tap at the door. "Kyle?"

"Yeah."

Mom's face appeared. "Bri told me what happened."

"He did?"

She nodded. Then she came over to my bed and sat

down. "Oh, Kyle, I'm so sorry. Whatever your father said to you, he didn't mean it. You know that, don't you, honey?"

I kept my face expressionless. "Sure," I said. "No problem."

"It's his job. Everything's on the line right now. He's taking his problems out on you. On us. That doesn't make it okay, I know." Mom sighed. "But things will get better, I promise."

"They will? When?"

Mom didn't answer. She began smoothing down the cowlick that made my hair stick up on top. After a moment she stopped and patted my cheek. "Trust me on this one, Kyle. Okay?"

But Mom, I wanted to shout, he called me a screw-up. He said things to his own kid you wouldn't say to your worst enemy. It's *not* okay.

But I didn't say anything. Mom looked so sad and tired, I figured that was the last thing she needed to hear. Instead, I leaned over and gave her a hug.

Finally she let go of me and stood up. "Your dad's in the bedroom, lying down. I'm going to start dinner. Want to help?"

"Sure," I said. I scrambled off the bed. "So, did you sell any condos today?"

She smiled. "A lot of people came and looked. But I think one couple was really interested. So keep your fingers crossed."

"Will do," I said. As I followed her down the stairs I put

my hand behind my back and crossed my fingers, really hard. But it had nothing to do with selling condos. Nothing at all.

CHAPTER 8

The next day I stayed late to watch Brian's practice; I didn't want to risk catching Dad home alone.

I sat in the high school bleachers while the team went through their plays. Bri was amazing. He'd float through the air like a human Frisbee, then turn and casually push the ball through the hoop, like the thought had just occurred to him.

"I'll never be able to play like you," I told him, when he came out of the showers.

"I could show you a few tricks."

"Don't bother," I said. "I'm Coach Simpson's mascot. The Wheaton Warriors' token shrimp."

Brian squinted at me. "So, ignore him. Anyway, basketball isn't the only game in town. Next year, try out for track. Coach Russell really works with his runners. You'd like it a lot."

"Yeah, but I bet Dad wouldn't," I muttered.

As we left the high school, Brian shot me a look. "Why do you let him push you around, Kyle?"

he asked. "You know what a bully he is when he gets like that. You've got to stick up for yourself!"

I stopped walking and stared at him. "What am I supposed to do? Punch him in the nose? Boy, that would solve everything!"

"That's not what I meant. But maybe it isn't such a bad idea." Brian scowled and kicked at a pebble. "You should have heard him last night when I told him to quit picking on you. 'You stay out of this, bla bla bla, this is between me and Kyle.' Yeah, right. How long did he stand there yelling at you, while you didn't say a word?"

All of a sudden I did get mad, but not at Dad. "Listen, I can take care of myself. You don't have to treat me like I'm some helpless baby whose diapers need changing."

Brian's face twisted into a grin. "Well, gee, I'm glad to hear that, Squirt." He paused and sniffed. "You sure they don't need changing?"

I chased him all the way home.

Just the same, I stayed upstairs doing my homework until dinner. All through the meal, I didn't say anything to Dad. He seemed more interested in his mashed potatoes anyway. That was fine with me.

The standoff ended on Friday. Dad was waiting in the driveway when I got home. The trunk of the Taurus was open, and I could see something poking out of it.

I watched Dad wrestle a big box out of the trunk and set it down in the driveway. Then he opened the car door and unloaded more boxes from the back seat.

Dad's face was beaded with sweat as he bent over and reached for the biggest box. "Grab one end, okay, Kyle?" he called.

I picked up one side of the box. It weighed a ton. "What's in here?" I asked. "Weight-lifting equipment?"

Dad laughed, but he sounded sort of breathless. Yanking, lifting, and tugging, we dragged everything out to the patio. Then Dad stood back and wiped his hands on his pantlegs. "That," he said, after a few deep breaths, "is your new pool."

I looked at the boxes. Then I looked at Dad. "You're kidding."

"Nope. Just add water, it says. Some light assembly may be required." He smiled, waiting.

I didn't say anything. For some reason, all I could picture were those bouquets of flowers that showed up the day after Mom's birthday.

"We'll have to wait until next summer to put it up," I said finally.

"Still feels like summer to the old man." Dad looked hopefully up at the blue sky. "Anyway, it's a portable pool. Set it up, fill it, and then when the weather changes, you can take it down and stash it in the garage."

"Oh," I said. I looked at the box again. On the side was a picture of the assembled pool full of happy, laughing people. The picture made it look bigger than the pool down at the Y.

Dad put his hands together and rubbed them. "So," he said, "maybe this weekend, you and me and Bri could take a crack at putting this baby together. Just to give it a test run. Sound like a plan?"

"Sure, Dad," I said. "And then, once it's up, maybe I can invite Rowena over to try it out."

His face broke into a relieved smile. "Great idea, Kyle! We'll invite the whole neighborhood. Have a big Maxwell pool party, compliments of the owner here." And he clapped me on the back, like I'd won a big prize or something.

But Dad wasn't finished. He waited until Mom and Brian got home, and everyone had finished oohing and aahing over the portable pool. The picture of it on the box, anyway. Then he went over to Mom and put his arm around her.

"Honey, you've put in a hard week. What do you say we skip dinner tonight, and I take everybody out to the Edgartown ball park. Hot dogs all around!"

I perked up at that. The Edgartown Eagles were a local minor league baseball team. They were about as minor as you could get, short of Little League, but it was still fun to root for your team and eat plenty of junk food.

Mom laughed. "I think the Eagles are a little more excitement than I can stand. Why don't you take the boys?"

"Spoil sport," Dad said, but he smiled when he said it. He turned to Bri and me. "Okay, guys, grab your jackets. We don't want to miss the national anthem."

I was ready to head for the stairs. But Brian just stood there on the patio, digging the toe of his sneaker into the flagstones. "Think I'll pass," he said.

I stared at him. "Aw, c'mon, Bri. We haven't been to an Eagles game all summer!"

He shook his head, looking down at his feet. "Nah, I got stuff to do."

"Now, Bri." Dad pretended to look stern. "One party pooper's plenty. You don't want to let down the team, do you?"

"Please, Bri?"

Finally Brian raised his head. I fixed him with a long, pleading look. After a moment, he sighed. "Okay. If it's that big a deal . . ."

"Good." Dad clapped his hands together briskly. "The game bus departs in precisely ten minutes." He turned to Mom. "Sure I can't talk you into coming, Betsy? We're playing the Altoona White Sox."

Mom grinned. "Now, there's an offer I can refuse. No, I thought I might set up my easel. Get some painting done in peace and quiet for a change."

"Art before baseball?" Dad shook his head in disbelief. Then he tapped his watch. "All right, guys, shake a leg there."

I followed Brian up the stairs to get my jacket. But when we reached the hall, he dragged me into the bathroom and slammed the door shut.

"Great! Just great! The last thing I wanted to do tonight was get stuck with *him* and his Father of the Year routine. Thanks a lot, Kyle!" Brian glared at me. Then he turned away and pretended to be busy washing his hands at the sink.

I gaped at him. "It's just a ball game, Bri. I . . . I thought it would be more fun if we all went, that's all."

Brian splashed his hands under the tap. "I can't believe you still fall for those bribes," he muttered. "Why don't you just tell him to take his presents and his ball games and—"

"Because I can't!"

Brian turned off the water. "Why not?" he asked. "You're just playing into his game. If Dad has a problem with alcohol, that's not your fault, Kyle. And it's not mine. It's his."

He really looked sorry for me when he said that. For some reason, it infuriated me.

"So he has a few drinks once in a while! So what? I've seen Rowena's dad do the same thing." I knew what I was saying was wrong, that Dad had a problem, but I couldn't stop myself. Once Referee Mode kicked in, it was like somebody else took over my brain, and I found myself stuck between Dad and Brian, whether I liked it or not.

But Brian just shook his head. "It's not the same thing," he said.

I played my last card. "Yeah, well, I suppose it's not the same thing when your friends get hold of a six-pack and do some partying, huh, Brian?" He looked startled, but I forged ahead. "Come on, I know they do, because they brag about it to their brothers, and they all talk about it at school. Not to mention some even worse stuff!"

He was quiet for a moment. We could hear Dad yelling for us to get a move on. Finally Brian dried his hands and headed for the door. When we reached the hall, he looked back at me and shook his head. "It's not the same thing, Squirt. Someday you'll figure that out."

I didn't bother to argue.

The Edgartown Eagles weren't having much of a season. By the time we'd found a spot in the bleachers, and devoured two hot dogs apiece, the Eagles were down 0–8, and it was only the third inning.

"We want a pitcher, not a glass of water," the fans started chanting. It made me feel kind of bad for the pitcher, who was a red-headed stringbean of a guy. He had long, skinny legs like Rowena's but not half her strength.

Finally the Edgartown manager had enough. He came out and took the ball away from the pitcher, and the stringbean guy headed for the dugout. No one was warming up in the bullpen, which says a lot about the Eagles, considering they'd already given up eight runs.

Brian began talking to some girls in the bleachers next to us. Dad was craning his neck, checking out the crowd. All of a sudden he stood up and began waving at someone to join us.

"Who's that?" I asked, as a tall man with dark hair made his way through the stands. A tall, dark-haired kid was with him.

"That's Ken Hicks," Dad told me in a half-whisper. "My new supervisor. So sit up and do me proud, okay, Kyle?"

"Sure, Dad," I said. I straightened a little and waited until the man found our row. I watched Dad reach over and shake his hand. They talked about the game while the supervisor's kid sized me up. I was glad I was sitting down.

Then the man smiled at me. "This is my son, Joel," he said. "He'll be starting eighth grade over at Wheaton."

"No kidding?" Dad looked overjoyed. "Gee, Ken, I didn't know you were looking for a place right in town. You should have said something. My wife works for a realtor."

"Is that so?" The man smiled again, but he didn't look too excited about it. I kind of wished Dad would tone it down.

Then Dad turned to me. "Listen, Kyle here is in the eighth grade. He'll be glad to show your boy around. Won't you, Kyle?"

I nodded. The kid said nothing, but his dad looked pleased. "Great," he said. "It's pretty tough when you're starting at a new school. And we've started more than our share, right, Joel?"

The boy nodded, and a half smile crossed his face. Then Mr. Hicks glanced at his watch and back down at the field.

"Looks like they're ready to play ball," he said. "Listen, we'd better get back to our seats. But it was great to run into you and your boys, Jim. You have a fine family there."

Dad beamed. Then he snapped his supervisor a jokey little salute. "See you Monday, Ken," he said.

"Eight o'clock *sharp*," Mr. Hicks said, and they both laughed.

We watched the Hickses pick their way across the bleachers. When Dad turned back, he wasn't smiling anymore.

"There," he said, "goes our future. I'm serious, Kyle. We've got a lot riding on how well I impress that man. So

I want you to make sure his boy feels very welcome. Do you read me, son?"

"Loud and clear, Dad," I said.

"Good. Now, who wants another hot dog?"

By the time the Eagles landed, they'd used up every pitcher on the bench and were probably recruiting volunteers from the stands. Parents gathered up their kids and headed for the parking lot. I yawned and rubbed my stomach. My voice was hoarse from shouting; I'd eaten too many hot dogs; and the Eagles lost 13–zip. A classic night at the ball park.

Dad and Brian walked ahead, teeing off on the wretched Eagles. On our way to the car we saw Mr. Hicks and his son climbing into a shiny new van, and Dad gave them a big wave.

As the van pulled away I found myself waving too. I stared at the tinted windows. Whoever that kid was, he was about to get a new friend. Even if it killed me.

I could just hear Bri scoff. "Dad makes you miserable and then he turns around and asks you to do him a favor. Why do you bother?"

Because it's better than nothing, I thought. Because it's a way of helping instead of hurting. Because he's my dad, and he asked.

As we drove away from the park, I sat in the back seat and listened to Dad and Brian dissect the game. The two jocks were really going at it.

"Did you see that big dunce they had for a catcher? No way, man! Everything he couldn't handle he called a wild pitch. Like—every other pitch!"

Dad hooted. "They shouldn't call them the Eagles—the Edgartown Mudhens is more like it."

I smiled to myself in the dark. This was more like it. This was the way things were, before the Stranger came and all the trouble started. Back when everything in my life seemed perfect.

Then again, I might settle for slightly imperfect, I decided, squishing around in the seat to make room for those last two hot dogs. Compared with the pits, I'd settle for that any day.

CHAPTER 9

The trouble with perfect, of course, is that there's no such thing. But if there were, it would come with its own brand name, and that name would be Joel Hicks.

I got my first inkling of Joel's genius the day he showed up at Wheaton Junior High. It began with gym.

I changed into my grungies and headed out of the locker room. I felt terrible. Gym class first thing in the morning must be the reason coffee was invented, I figured, as Coach Simpson barked out our names and started us on laps. Right then, I decided that Coach Simpson must be the reason rat poison was invented.

Everyone hated doing laps, including Boyd the Bully. He did manage to stick out his foot so that Scott would trip over it and fall on his face. But even Boyd didn't have his usual nasty zip.

I was just about to ask if he'd forgotten to eat his parsley, when something grabbed Boyd's attention. He lifted his big head like a tiger sniffing meat, and trained it at the door of the locker room.

"Who's that?" he growled.

He was chewing two packs of Super-Bubble gum, a crime anyone but Pearson would get fifty sit-ups for, so the question sounded more like "Ooo aahrr?"

We'd reached home court. "What?" I said. Boyd pointed.

Coach Simpson had his hand on the shoulder of a tall, dark-haired kid. The kid was saying something, and Coach Simpson nodded and laughed. I saw it was Joel Hicks, the supervisor's son.

"New kid," I reported.

Boyd's beady eyes gleamed with anticipation. He practically smacked his lips. Making life miserable for new kids was one of Boyd's favorite pastimes, and everybody knew it. I saw the other guys glance at Joel, as they wondered what gruesome fate lay in store.

Coach Simpson's whistle pierced my brain. Today's class, he announced, would be gymnastics. That meant vaulting over the horse, climbing the rope, doing pull-ups, and jumping on the trampoline.

As we went through our paces, I kept my eye on Joel and Boyd. When it was Joel's turn to vault the horse, I saw Boyd pause next to the equipment. Sure enough, when Joel grabbed the top of the horse to push himself over, his hands stuck to it like glue.

Not glue, I thought, as he came crashing down on the other side. Try two packs of chewed-up Super-Bubble gum.

I watched Joel pick himself up and stare at his hands. After a moment, I went over to him.

"Don't worry," I said. "It's just gum. Compliments of the school bully."

Joel was rolling his palms together, trying to peel the gum off. "No kidding," he said. "I thought maybe it was top-secret army issue defoliant."

Then he looked up and grinned. "You're Kip or something, right? I saw you at the game the other night."

"Kyle," I said. "And you're Josh or something."

His grin got wider. "Joel," he said. "Joel Hicks. So, which one's the bully?"

"Three guesses." We made our way over to the rope, where Boyd was glowering massively.

"Well, it can't be you. And it can't be all these interested onlookers." Joel narrowed his eyes. "So my money goes on Godzilla over there."

"Bingo," I said.

Joel's blue eyes began to glitter. When Coach Simpson had finished his lecture on rope-climbing safety, Joel walked over to Boyd.

"We already did this at my last school," he said. "Allow me to demonstrate."

Boyd blinked. Before anyone could say "army issue defoliant," Joel had grabbed Boyd's hand, slapped the gum in it, and fixed it to the rope. "There you go, pal," he said. "First rule of safety: Don't fall."

Boyd opened his mouth to say something. Then he tried to move his hand. The gum moved with it.

Angrily Boyd grabbed the thick rope with his other

hand and started to pull himself up. A yard of Super-Bubble followed.

He tried again. Same result.

The whole class broke up. We giggled and chuckled and guffawed as Boyd Pearson flailed around on the gummy rope, until Coach Simpson ran over and started yelling about showing respect for the equipment.

Boyd stared at his bubble-gum umbilical cord while the coach got a rag full of rubbing alcohol and began swiping at the gum. Then he pronounced sentence: fifty sit-ups.

Boyd's head swiveled around. His eyes came to rest on the new kid. The look in them wasn't hard to read.

I didn't waste a second. "Boyd Pearson, meet Joel Hicks."

By now Boyd's eyes were angry little slits. He mumbled something under his breath. I thought I caught the word "death." Or maybe it was "kill."

Joel just smiled. "The pleasure," he said, "is all mine."

"That was awesome!" I shook my head in admiration. "I've been trying to get Boyd Pearson for years. You managed it on your first day!"

Joel shrugged. "When you've been to as many schools as I have, you learn about bullies, Kip. Believe me, they all look alike after a while."

We were sitting in the lunchroom. Boyd sat a few tables away, glowering into his meatloaf. Near the stage, the girls' whispering society was checking out the new kid. I saw

Celia peer over at our table. When she caught me watching her, her face got red and she quickly turned away.

I took a bite of my sandwich and swallowed. "How many?" I asked.

"How many what?" Joel was peering into his lunch bag like he'd never seen it before.

"Schools."

He took out his sandwich and unwrapped it. "Since kindergarten? Oh, maybe seven. Eight, if you count the last one."

Even someone who was terrible at math could figure that one out. It came to a school a year. "Wow," I said. "So, how come you wouldn't count the last one?"

"Because at the last one I got kicked out," Joel said. He bit into his sandwich and made a face. "Ugh. Liverwurst!"

I forced myself to finish my tuna fish. Then, as casually as I could, I asked, "What did you get kicked out for?" No one at Wheaton ever got expelled. They just had to do more sit-ups.

Joel reached into the bag again and took out an apple. "Personal differences," he answered. He paused. "I think that means they wished I was a different person."

That cracked me up. Joel grinned too, as he polished his apple on the front of his shirt. "But like I told the military academy, hey—I gotta be me." He took a big bite of his apple and sat there chewing.

"No, really," I persisted. "What happened?"

Joel squinted down at his apple. "Everybody at that place was like Pearson over there. You know, no-brainers.

Mouth-breathers. Jocks. They punished anyone who wasn't. I think you know what I'm talking about."

I nodded.

"My dad thought I'd like it because it was a boarding school and I was getting sick of moving around. We have to, because of my dad's job. He gets transferred all over the country. He's an efficiency expert. The company brings him in when their branches don't make enough money."

I nodded again. Joel sounded like quite the expert himself. "So what does he do, exactly?"

"He gets rid of the dead wood," Joel said offhandedly.

All of a sudden I was sorry I'd asked. He meant his father fired people. Like the guys in Dad's office.

I began unwrapping my cookies. Joel was watching me, chewing on his apple. I took my time, hoping he'd get the hint and change the subject.

Finally Joel tossed the apple core into his lunch bag and crumpled it up. "Hey, I didn't mean your father or anything, Maxwell," he said. "Come on. I can't help what my dad does for a living any more than you can. Okay?"

"Yeah. Okay."

Joel smiled. "Great," he said. "Now that we're pals again, who's that weird-looking girl heading straight for our table?"

I didn't have to turn around. "You mean Rowena Whipple?"

"You tell me."

Even if I could have summed up Rowena in thirty seconds, I didn't get the chance. She screeched to a halt next to my chair. "Where were you, Kyle? We were supposed to go over math together. Today. At lunch."

I stared down at my uneaten cookies. "I—uh—"

While Rowena was fixing me with a withering stare, I saw Joel glance at her. His eyes took in her stringy black hair and noodly legs and angry expression.

Then he gave her a big smile. "Hi," he said. "I'm Joel. This is my first day here, and Kyle was showing me around."

"Yes," I said, "I was showing Joel around. And I'm sorry I forgot about the math. Can't we do it after school?"

Rowena didn't blink. "Pleased to meet you," she said in a flat voice. She turned back to me. "And no, we can't do it after school. I have to babysit the Rat, and if you think I'm going to try to explain isosceles triangles with Arnold around, you're nuts."

With an angry toss of her black hair, Rowena stomped off.

Joel pushed back his chair. "Whew," he said. "Not very friendly, is she?"

"She is, once you get to know her," I assured him. I was about to add, "Besides, she's my best friend," but Joel's eyes were busy scanning the lunchroom. They grazed past Boyd and settled on Celia's table. We watched the girls get up and move in a big pack down the aisle.

"Listen," Joel said, once they were gone, "since you don't have to study after school, why don't you show me around town? I haven't seen much since we moved in. My mom's been too busy unpacking stuff."

"Sure," I said. "Except there isn't much to see. The Fox River Mall, a couple of movie theaters, and some stores downtown. I don't know where you lived before, but I doubt Wheaton will seem like much of a treat. It's pretty, well, average."

"Average is great," Joel said, with a big smile. He broke off part of my chocolate chip cookie, and popped it in his mouth. "Average is absolutely—perfect."

On the way to the mall, Joel told me he'd lived in Cleveland, St. Louis, Houston, and New York City. "And a bunch of other places," he added. "But I was pretty little then. They all start to blur after a while."

I thought of telling him about my own big adventure, when Scott and I ran away to Lewistown, but I decided not to. Eating bologna in a park doesn't exactly compare to living in New York City on the excitement scale.

Neither did the Fox River Mall. It was about a mile from Wheaton Center, and it had one major department store, a drugstore outlet, some sporting goods places, and a Mr. Frostee. But Joel seemed to like it fine.

We walked around for a while. Then we stopped and got a milkshake. Joel told me about his brother, who was in college. "Sometimes I really miss having Pete around. I think my parents do too. Especially my dad. He's gotten a lot more strict with just me at home. Plus he's been drinking more, too."

I stared at Joel. I couldn't believe the way he

just tossed that off, to someone he hardly knew.

At the same time, I kind of admired the way he'd said it. No code of silence, no referee whistle in the distance. Just the facts, ma'am.

Suddenly Joel gave me a nudge. "Look who's here."

It was Boyd. He was prowling past the Foot Locker, his big paws shoved in his pockets, his lips puffed out menacingly.

"Let's get out of here," I suggested. Joel followed me past the ice cream counter and across the mall to the department store.

As we walked through the men's department, I told Joel about my history with Boyd. He whistled when I got to the part about the basketball team.

"He plays center? You're kidding! He looks about as fast as a tree stump."

"You met Coach Simpson. Figure it out."

Joel groaned and shook his head. When we saw Pearson coming, we cruised past the cosmetics section and then ducked out the back end of the store.

"Wonder why he wasn't at practice," I said, as we started toward the main drag of Wheaton.

"Fifty sit-ups," Joel reminded me, and we both laughed.

By the time we reached the Texaco station, I felt better than I had in a long time. I glanced over at Joel. Maybe Dad was right, I thought. Maybe Joel and I could be friends. We sure seemed to have a lot in common.

When we got to the corner, Joel reached in his pocket

and pulled something out. "Here," he said. "I got you a present."

I looked at what he was holding. It was a leather wallet. The price tag was still on it. Even without touching it, I could tell it was expensive.

I could also tell something else. Joel hadn't paid for it. He couldn't have. We'd been together the whole time, and I never once saw him stop and buy anything.

Right then, all of my friendly feelings froze up tighter than a winter pond. I looked at the wallet and then at Joel Hicks.

"Thanks," I said. "But I've already got a wallet. You keep it."

"No, really," he insisted. "It's yours. I want you to have it, Kyle. Hey, we're friends, aren't we?"

How do you accuse someone you just met of shoplifting? Someone you like, even? And what if they deny it? Do you call them a liar?

Whatever you're supposed to do, I don't think it's covered in any advice columns. None I've ever read, anyway.

So I did the only thing I could think of. I thanked Joel, stuck the wallet in my jacket, and told him to wait while I ran into the gas station to use the bathroom.

I closed the rusty door to the men's room. Carefully, I took out the wallet, peeled off its price tag, and set it down on the washstand. I took a deep breath and counted to ten. Then I left.

Some gas station attendant was going to be happy

when he cleaned up the rest rooms that night. Whoever he was, I envied him. Because even though I liked Joel and we seemed to be hitting it off, and it was almost worth it to see Boyd Pearson grunt his way through fifty sit-ups, I was starting to wish I'd never met Joel Hicks.

CHAPTER
10

Dinner that night was my favorite: pork chops, with chocolate cake for dessert. I was about to get another piece of cake when Dad glanced up. "Just a moment there, champ."

"Yeah, Dad?"

"Ken Hicks said his kid started school today. He make out all right?"

"Fine," I said. "We had lunch together. After school I took him to the mall."

A big smile spread across Dad's face. "That's great, Kyle," he said. "I'm very happy to hear that. Looks like you made a friend today, huh?"

"Yeah, I guess it does." I decided to skip the cake. Then I excused myself before Dad could ask me any more questions.

I grabbed my math books and headed over to Rowena's. I wondered if I should tell her about the wallet. Then I decided not to. She'd probably ask me why I just didn't return it, and I wasn't sure what I'd say, except that I'm not the type that makes waves.

Besides, I was pretty sure when she'd said, "Pleased to meet you," that Rowena hadn't been pleased to meet Joel at all.

She didn't waste time confirming it. "Who was that creep you were sitting with at lunch?" she demanded to know as soon as she opened the door.

"Hi," I said. "Mind if I come in first?"

Grudgingly, she held the door open. The living room was full of older Whipple kids watching a sci-fi movie on TV. There was a lot of hooting and popcorn tossing going on. It looked like fun. But Rowena pointed grimly at the stairs.

"We have to be quiet," she said when we reached the hall. "Mom just got the Rat to go to bed."

"*Quiet?* With that demolition derby down there?"

Rowena gave me a stern glance, so I shut up and followed her into her room. "So who was that creep you were sitting with at lunch?" she repeated.

"His name's Joel Hicks. He's a new kid. And he really creamed Pearson in gym. You should have seen it!"

"I didn't like him," Rowena said. "He looked like a phony to me."

I sighed. "Well, I think he's okay. Besides, you don't even know him."

"Oh, and you do?"

Instead of answering, I covered my face with my hands and began to scream quietly.

Rowena watched me for a moment. Then she shook her head, sighed, and reached for the math books.

"Okay, Kyle. I'll give you the benefit of the doubt. *This* time. Just don't skip any more study sessions. There's stuff I'd rather be doing than explaining theorems to a hopeless case like you, you know."

"Cross my heart." I lowered my hands and tried to look grateful while Rowena sat down on the bed and opened the first book.

A half hour later I didn't feel grateful anymore.

"Whoa! Slow down! I'm not following any of this!"

Rowena looked up from the fiendish equation. "Well, if you'd let me explain it to you, maybe you would be able to follow it."

"So start explaining!"

"I'm trying to, Kyle. Honestly, if you can memorize history dates, why can't you memorize formulas? They're so simple!" Her patience was starting to wear thin.

"It's not the same thing," I said, as she brandished a page of trapezoids and octagons. "History's easy. You don't have to multiply the Battle of Hastings times the War of the Roses to find out what Joan of Arc ate for breakfast."

"Ky-uhl." Rowena sighed. "You should try to have a better attitude."

But my attitude wasn't the problem. By the end of our first study session, we both agreed the problem was my defective brain. "I want to understand this junk, honest! But the minute you make me use it in a problem, something gets—stuck."

"Don't worry," Rowena said. "It'll unstick. By the time

we take the test, you'll have the hang of it."

I thought she was being ridiculously optimistic, but I didn't say so. Rowena scribbled down a few scary-looking formulas and told me to look them over before I went to bed.

"Great," I said. "I'll probably have nightmares about a giant trapezoid trying to reduce me to a fraction."

Rowena gazed at me. "Good," she said. "Don't forget to study."

Class dismissed. "I won't," I told her, and picked up the list of math formulas. I folded it and shoved it in my pants pocket.

I didn't see it again until laundry day, when my mom took the pants out of the dryer. By then, the formulas were pretty hard to read. But I already had something else to worry about. Something a lot more terrifying than $A = \pi \times r^2$.

Mr. Campbell taught Music Appreciation. He seemed awfully young, hardly older than Brian. I could see why he'd gotten the job, though, because he sure appreciated music more than any person I'd ever met. He hummed while he wrote assignments on the blackboard. He went into a hypnotic trance when he played tapes of his favorite composers. His voice thundered out as he led us in singing folk songs. It was positively embarrassing.

One time he made us sing this Scottish song—a "bal-lade," Mr. Campbell called it—with the worst lyrics you could ever make a room full of eighth-graders sing.

Especially the guys. "Oh, Charlie is my darling, my darling, my darling! Charlie is my darling, the young cavalierrrr!" Mr. Campbell boomed out in his huge baritone, swinging his fist with gusto.

Scott and I exchanged glances. No way we were singing about some guy named Charlie being our darling. Or anyone else, for that matter. Mr. Campbell could just lump it.

But we did. We all sang it, even this kid named Charlie Bates, who sat at the front of the room with his ears turning red. Mostly we let the girls sing, while the rest of us kind of lip-synched the "darling" part.

Except for Boyd Pearson. I could hear him cackling from the back row as he and a couple of his pals came up with some new lyrics. "Charlie rides a Harley, a Harley, a Harley . . ." It would have been funny if Boyd hadn't dreamed it up.

But I couldn't blame Mr. Campbell. After all, this was his job, and he was definitely putting a lot into it. Besides, listening to music—*any* kind of music—made him so happy, you kind of hated to begrudge him his big pleasure in life.

Still, I wasn't prepared for what happened on Wednesday.

When I walked into school, I found Joel Hicks outside the music room, talking to Celia. He waved when he saw me.

"Kip," he yelled. "Over here, Kip."

I walked over to where they were standing.

"We were just talking about school clubs," Joel said. "Celia said I should join the Knowledge Bowl team. She said you could fill me in."

I looked at Celia. I hadn't talked to her since the zipper fiasco. In fact, I'd been avoiding her.

But she gave me a nice smile, and nodded encouragingly. I looked at Celia's slightly crooked teeth and shiny blond hair, and stifled a sigh. "Sure," I said. "You can come to our next meeting. It's today, after school."

"Great!" Joel turned and trained his killer smile on Celia. "His name's not really Kip, you know. I just call him that as a kind of joke."

"I know what his name is," Celia said. "It's Kyle." To my surprise, her face turned bright pink. Before I could say anything, the bell rang, and the three of us headed into Mr. Campbell's class.

The topic for the next two weeks was musicals. Mr. Campbell loved musicals even more than ballades. In his opinion, Rodgers and Hammerstein were the greatest things since Twinkies and milk. He played a bunch of songs from his favorite shows, belting out the words while Scott and I drew pictures of jet fighters flying in formation.

All of a sudden the music stopped.

"All right, class," Mr. Campbell said. "As you know, musicals are more than words and music. What makes them special, makes them come alive, are the performances. I want each one of you to experience the tradition that made these great shows part of our musical heritage."

Scott poked me. "What's he talking about?"

I shrugged. "Beats me." I added some insignia to my F-14 Tomcat.

"In that spirit," Mr. Campbell continued, "I'm splitting the class into groups. Each group will be assigned a particular show. You'll pick a producer and select some songs for the class. You can lip-synch to the soundtrack, but I want to see some great performances. I think we'll all have a lot of fun, and also learn something about musical theater. At least, that's the hope."

He started calling out names. When I looked up from my drawing, the unassigned kids had dwindled to a very small pool. Practically a puddle.

"And finally, group five will be doing *South Pacific*. Pearson, Kenyon, Maxwell, Hargrave, Goodman . . ."

I looked at Scott. Both of us peered over at Boyd. Scott turned back and mouthed the words "oh no." There wasn't much doubt who the producer was going to be.

Joel Hicks was standing across the room next to Celia. They were both in the *Oklahoma* group. I had a crummy feeling Joel would end up playing the hero. It didn't improve my mood.

Mr. Campbell was rushing from group to group, explaining how to cast the shows. "Okay," he said, when he reached our corner. "Now, *South Pacific* is set during World War Two. Most of the cast are sailors, which should work just fine, since we've got a lot of boys here. Which means, Marcy, you'll be Nellie Forbush, our intrepid heroine."

Marcy beamed.

Then Mr. Campbell frowned. "Only one problem. Who's left to play Bloody Mary?"

"Who's Bloody Mary?" Boyd asked.

"A big, humorous Polynesian woman who sings 'Bali Ha'i,' about a mythical island in the Pacific. A wonderful song, and a very important character in the show."

"What does Bloody Mary wear, exactly?" Boyd asked, his forehead wrinkling, like he really took this producing thing seriously.

"Oh, a tropical dress of some kind, I should think. Maybe a flower in her hair," Mr. Campbell said.

Boyd smiled. It was a lazy, satisfied smile, showing all of Boyd's pointy little teeth.

"Don't worry, Mr. Campbell," he said. "I think I know just the person we can get for Bloody Mary. Flowers and the whole bit. No problem!"

He was looking right at me.

CHAPTER 11

When the bell rang Boyd was still grinning at me. "Don't forget, Maxwell," he said. "Next week. You'd better be ready."

I saw Celia look over her shoulder and stop at the door, like she was waiting for me to catch up. I pretended to straighten my books until I was sure she'd left.

After school I introduced Joel to Ms. Loomis. We sat down next to Rowena. She shot Joel a long look, but at least she didn't say anything about phony creeps.

As soon as everyone showed up, Ms. Loomis gave us some sample tests to take. I creamed the literature section. But the math test was a disaster.

At the end of the meeting, Ms. Loomis called me up to her desk.

"Kyle," she said, tapping the math test, "this isn't what I'd hoped for. Didn't you and Rowena promise to study together?"

"We did," I said. "I guess it didn't do me much good, huh?"

She shook her head. "I've been counting on you to

anchor this team, Kyle. But unless you can manage a passing score in math, you might not make the team at all."

Then her face relaxed. "Well, we don't want that to happen, do we? So let's start hitting the books, okay?"

Joel was waiting for the late bus when I got outside. "What's the matter, Kip? You look like your dog just died."

"Not my dog—*me*," I muttered. "That math is going to be murder."

Joel laughed. "Listen, don't sweat math. I never studied a day in my life, and I always pass. You just have to have the right attitude."

"Really?" I said. "How do I get the right attitude?"

Joel glanced around. Then he leaned toward me. "Think positive," he said. "Now, quit frowning. That math test is going to be a breeze. Trust me."

It didn't help. All the way home, I worried, and not just about Ms. Loomis. What would Dad say if I screwed up? It was bad enough not making the basketball team.

"Time to start hitting the books, buddy." I swiped at a rock with my foot and gave it a sharp kick. Too bad Wheaton didn't have a soccer team, I thought, as the rock landed down the block. Then I realized that was dumb. Even if it did, Bri would probably be the captain.

When I got home, I stopped in the kitchen to make myself some molasses milk. I'd read that the iron in molasses makes your bones grow. Whether it did or not, it tasted excellent.

I reached in the cupboard where Mom stored her baking stuff, and then my hand froze. The top shelf, where Dad kept his bottles, was empty.

I felt around to make sure. Then I crawled up on the counter and took a peek. A huge grin spread across my face. No gin, no whiskey, no vodka. This time he meant it, I was sure. No more drinking, no more cruddy Stranger wrecking things for everybody. There was the sweet, beautiful proof—a whole foot of space in the kitchen cupboard.

After I made the molasses milk I headed upstairs to listen to *South Pacific*. Mr. Campbell had made tapes so that everyone could practice their songs.

I played "Bali Ha'i" a couple of times, while I stared at the words on the hand-out sheet. Mr. Campbell was right about one thing—it was sure a nice song. And if I were a big, humorous Polynesian lady, I'd be thrilled to sing it.

But I wasn't a Polynesian lady. Or even big. And the last thing I wanted to do was stand up in front of Joel and Celia and the entire Music Appreciation class, and hear the roar of their laughter. And worst of all, know it was Boyd's idea.

But next week, that's exactly what was going to happen. I was doomed.

"Kyle?" Dad stuck his head around the door.

I scrambled into an upright position. "Yeah, Dad?"

"Just wondered if you'd seen my calculator." Dad glanced around the room. He was about to leave when he spotted the lyric sheet. "Hey, *South Pacific*. What a great show!"

He picked up the hand-out with a smile. "I remember

going to see this movie when I was about your age," he said, staring down at the words. "Well, maybe a little younger. They sure don't make musicals like they used to."

"No, I guess not," I said.

"What's this for? A school assignment?"

"Yeah."

Dad nodded. "Well, I won't interrupt your studying. Guess I'll have to find that calculator myself."

He was halfway to the door when I blurted, "Dad? Can I ask you a question?"

He paused. "Sure, Kyle. Fire away."

"Did you ever make a total fool of yourself, in front of a whole bunch of people, and there was no way of getting out of it?"

The question caught him by surprise. For a minute he frowned, like he was trying to figure out if there was some trick answer to it. Then he began to smile.

"Of course I have, Kyle. We all have. I can think of at least two sales presentations that were complete, total disasters, and there was nothing I could do but grin and bear it."

He shook his head. "Even had a whole projector tip over on me once. I had all my figures written on a transparency and it fell onto the light bulb and . . . melted."

"So, like, after it happened, did it seem funny to you? It didn't haunt you for the rest of your life?"

Dad peered at me. "Is there something I'm missing here, Kyle? Are you in some kind of trouble?"

I sighed. "No," I said. "It's just that we're doing these songs for music class . . . and I have to be Bloody Mary and wear a dress and flowers in my hair. I'll be the biggest joke in the eighth grade!"

Dad scratched his head. Then he smiled. "Kyle, I sympathize. But if this is the worst thing that ever happens to you, you'll lead a charmed life, believe me. The important thing is to show the class you know it's a joke. If they think you're in on it, they won't be laughing at you—they'll be on your side."

"So how am I supposed to do that?"

"Play it to the hilt. Wear your costume like a badge of honor!" He came over and sat down on the bed. "Remember that movie *Tootsie*? When Dustin Hoffman dressed up like a woman because he needed an acting job?"

I nodded. We'd rented the video a couple of times. I never thought it would become the story of my life.

"So, it was a great movie, right? The guy took a ridiculous situation and made it work for him. Trust me, that's the attitude to have."

I groaned. "Dad, there is no way I can make this *work* for me! Besides, what about the song? It doesn't make any sense! I've looked at it a million times, and all I can figure is that it's about a talking volcano."

Dad picked up the words to "Bali Ha'i" and read them to himself. After a minute, he looked over at me.

"Okay, I'll give it a try. The song says that everybody lives on a lonely island of some kind or another, but we all have this special place we'd like to escape to. Except we can't get there, see, because maybe it doesn't really exist."

For a moment I wasn't sure if Dad was talking about the song or something else. He had a funny expression on his face, as if he were trying to explain something he couldn't put into words.

"See, it's not really about an island, Kyle. It says that everybody has hopes and dreams, and you have to believe you can achieve them, even if they seem very far away. Or maybe even . . . impossible."

I swear, I'd read that song over and over, and I sure hadn't gotten any of that stuff out of it. Then again, maybe it helped if you'd seen the movie.

Dad was still gazing at the sheet of lyrics. He shook his head. "Nope," he said. "They sure don't make musicals like they used to."

The moment of truth had arrived. Showtime at the Wheaton Junior High Corral.

First we sat through Judy Bonner as the King of Siam, dressed in her father's silk pajamas while she waltzed Meredith Donnelly around to "Shall We Dance?" I stared at the floor while Joel and Celia sat on the piano bench and lip-synched "People Will Say We're In Love." Then it was our group's turn.

At our only rehearsal no one had brought a costume. A feeling of suspense hovered over us as we left to change.

In the boys' room the Seabees peeled down to T-shirts and pulled on white sailor caps. They were set to go.

Boyd, who was playing Emile, the French plantation owner, stood at the mirror tying a scarf around his throat. We all covered our ears while he bellowed out a verse from "Some Enchanted Evening."

"I think you got it wrong, Pearson," I said, when he stopped for breath. "An evening with you wouldn't be enchanted—it'd be *haunted.*"

All the Seabees hooted at that one. Boyd shot me a look of disgust. "So where's your costume, Maxwell?" he demanded. "Because, I'm warning you, you'd better have one."

"Don't worry, it's right here. I'll be out in a sec."

Gripping my paper bag, I went into one of the cubicles and opened the bag. Inside was a polyester housecoat covered with purple and yellow flowers. One of Rowena's aunts had bought it in Hawaii. It had pink ruffles around the bottom and gigantic sparkly buttons.

I pulled on the housecoat. Then I took one of Mom's yellow chrysanthemums out of the bag and pinned it in my hair.

"Okay, Tootsie," I muttered. "Take it like a man." Squaring my shoulders, I stepped out of the cubicle.

Silence greeted me. The only sound was the rustle of my housecoat as I walked over to the mirror. I could see Boyd standing behind me. His mouth had dropped open. Awe, I told myself. The big goon was totally awestruck.

I reached into my pocket and pulled out a crimson lipstick Rowena had swiped from her mom. Slowly I smeared it on my mouth. I could feel the shudders as I added a second coat for good measure.

I stood back and adjusted the chrysanthemum. "Well? What do you think?"

Scott shook his head. "You're nuts, Kyle. Totally, completely out there." But he gave me an admiring punch on the shoulder.

Boyd still hadn't said a word. I walked over until I stood a few inches from his nose. "Aren't you going to say anything, Pearson? After all, this was your big idea."

"Get away from me!" he said in alarm. "Kenyon's right, you're nuts!"

"Stark raving nuts," I agreed. To prove it, I leaned over and planted a big crimson smooch on his cheek. Boyd let out a roar and grabbed his face. But it was too late. We could hear Mr. Campbell telling us to get ready. Curtain time.

I waited in the hall while the Seabees did their number and then Boyd and Marcy moved their lips to "Some Enchanted Evening." When I heard the dramatic opening notes of "Bali Ha'i" I took a deep breath and straightened my housecoat. I licked my crimson lips. Then I opened the door and walked into the music room.

The biggest wave of laughter I've ever heard erupted from every corner of the room. I could hardly hear the tape, but I focused on the song. I gave it everything I had. I even added some inspired hip movements, as the pink ruffles swayed around my legs.

Maybe it was the costume. Maybe it was the music. Maybe it was the tears of laughter that streamed down Mr.

Campbell's cheeks. But when I finished, the laughter had turned to cheers.

Bloody Mary had brought down the house.

CHAPTER 12

Rowena was waiting out in the hall. I could tell she'd been watching, but she didn't let on.

"Here." I handed her the bag with the costume inside. "Tell your aunt some of those buttons are coming loose."

"Sorry about the lipstick," she said. "I should have warned you it doesn't come off."

"I noticed," I said. No matter how hard I scrubbed, I still looked like I'd eaten ten cherry Popsicles.

"Try some cold cream," Rowena suggested.

"No thanks," I told her. "As of this moment, my life as a girl is officially over."

Maybe so, but all the way to the cafeteria, kids kept coming up to say how funny I'd looked or how much they loved my Bloody Mary routine. Wait'll I tell Dad, I thought. I took his advice—and it worked!

When we reached the door of the lunchroom, I spotted Celia Simkewicz at the end of the hot-food line.

Rowena saw her too. "So, have you talked to her yet?" she asked sternly.

"Kind of." I didn't feel like going into the zipper fiasco.

"Well, now's your chance."

"No, I don't think—" Then I saw Joel Hicks move toward the lunch line. Wetting my cherry-Popsicle lips, I took a few steps and ended up right behind Celia.

"Hi," I said.

She turned around. "Oh hi, Kyle. Hey, you were great today in music class. I thought I was going to die laughing!"

"It was that lethal, huh?"

We began to move down the line. Today's special was macaroni and cheese. It looked pretty putrid, but the other stuff looked even worse. Celia and I each took a plate and put it on our trays.

"You'd think they never heard of hamburgers in this place," I said, staring at the bright orange mound.

"No kidding." Celia sighed. "I just love bacon burgers, don't you? With cheese and pickles. Mmm!"

Cheese and pickles . . . For some reason, "Some Enchanted Evening" began bouncing around in my head. Let me tell you, that Rodgers and Hammerstein stuff can really rub off on a guy. All those cowboys and sailors and Siamese kings falling in love all over the place.

Which might explain what happened next. Before I could stop it, something weird was coming out of my mouth. Something I couldn't believe I'd ever say.

"Celia? How'd you like to come over after school and have a bacon burger?"

Celia looked kind of shocked. Which was the way I felt.

"My mom makes these great hamburgers," I heard the weird kid who'd taken over my body say. "She puts chili and stuff on them. Bacon, too, of course. They're really, uh, great."

We'd reached the end of the line where the cashier sat. Celia was staring down at her plate of moldy macaroni like it was about to attack her.

Maybe it was me she was worried about. I didn't blame her. I had just invited Celia Simkewicz over to my house. Scott was right. I must be nuts.

Finally Celia handed the cashier a lunch ticket and looked back at me.

"I have cheerleading practice after school today," she said. "My mom comes and picks me up so I don't have to take the bus."

It wasn't a "yes." But it wasn't a "no," either.

"I could wait until your practice is over." A strange determination suddenly gripped me. "Then you can ask your mom if it's okay. My brother could give you a ride home. You live in the north end, right?"

Celia looked surprised, but she nodded. "So," she asked, "is your brother the Brian Maxwell who won all those games for Wheaton High last year?"

I sighed. "Yeah. Not much family resemblance, is there?"

Celia squinted up her eyes. "No, not really." She paused, while my heart took a dive. Then she added, "For one thing, you wear a *lot* more lipstick."

I cracked up when she said that, mostly from relief. She could have said a million other things, but I was glad she hadn't.

I waited while she picked up her tray. Then I said, "Well, what about it? Think you can come?"

Celia thought about it. Then she smiled. "If you can wait until practice is over, I'll ask my mom. Okay?"

"Okay!" I started walking toward a nearby table, where Rowena was unpacking her lunch.

"And where do you think you're going?"

The cashier was frowning at me. "Do you have a ticket for that meal, young man?" she asked. "Lunches aren't free, you know!"

I turned redder than my lipstick. The kids in line were all snickering at me. I checked to see whether Celia had noticed. But she had already left to sit with her pals by the stage, to tell them what she thought of Kyle Henry Maxwell, the Bloody Mary Kid.

"Kyle?" Mom said. "What's that noise? Where are you?"

The pay phone was right outside the gym. I had to cup a hand over my ear to hear.

"I'm at school. Watching basketball practice." Then I paused. "How come you're home? No houses for sale this week?"

She laughed. "Not quite. Mary Ellen Baker commissioned some more flower designs. Remember those chrysanthemums? She loved them. So I'm trying something new. Oils, this time. I thought some big sunflowers would—"

"Mom," I interrupted, "that's really interesting. But I need to ask you something. It's a favor, sort of."

"What kind of favor?"

Coach Simpson's whistle blasted my eardrums. "Mom," I practically shouted, "do you think you could make hamburgers tonight?"

"Well, sure, honey, but . . . "

"And make a couple extra, okay? I invited someone over."

"Anyone I know?" Mom suddenly sounded interested. "Is it Ken Hicks's son, by any chance?"

"No, Mom. It's a girl. And I promised her a ride home, so I hope Dad isn't going to be late tonight."

I prayed she wasn't going to ask a bunch of dumb questions, like, "Where did you meet this girl?" or "Do I know her parents?" Or even, "You didn't tell me you had a girlfriend."

But Mom was cool. "Well, if he is, Bri can take the station wagon," she said. "Now, how does your guest like her hamburgers? With cheese or without?"

Tweet! The whistle blasted again. Coach Simpson began screaming at the Warriors. "Mom, I got to go. But—maybe with some bacon, okay? And some pickles. I think pickles would be good." I suddenly felt nervous. Panicky, actually. Soon Celia Simkewicz would be sinking her slightly crooked teeth into my mom's cooking.

That is, if her mom said yes.

I went back to the gym with a worried heart. I sat in the bleachers wondering why Brian was so good at dealing with girls and I was so terrible. Well, maybe not terrible. But so far this sure wasn't what I'd call enjoyable.

I wondered if it would ever be. Those musical composers could write all the "boy meets girl" songs they wanted, but right then, all I felt was fear. And fear doesn't make you want to whistle a happy tune.

And then practice was over, and Celia was waving her pom-poms at me, and big old Boyd was peering over to take a look. And the fear went away, just like that. I waved back, and nodded when Celia pointed at the locker room, to tell me she had to go change.

By now Boyd was boiling with curiosity, but I just ignored him. I watched Celia disappear through the door. Then I leaned back against the bleachers to wait.

A funny feeling came over me while I waited. I figured this was how Dad felt when Mom was getting ready to go out for dinner. He'd gripe about being late, but he always looked happy and proud when she came down, all fixed up with earrings and lipstick and stuff.

I'd never waited for a girl before. It was definitely a personal feeling: It had to do with Celia and me, no one else. So I sat there waiting for Celia Simkewicz, and it felt pretty good.

Mrs. Simkewicz looked like an older version of Celia. Same hair, same teeth, same nice smile. She unrolled the car window while Celia told her about the bacon burger invitation. Then she peered over at me.

"Hi there, Kyle," Mrs. Simkewicz said. "I'm glad to meet you. And yes, Celia may have dinner at your house, so long as she leaves in time to do her homework." Then she offered to give us a ride over to my house.

"That's okay," I said. "It's only a few blocks. I walk to

school every day." I told her the address, so she wouldn't think I was a kidnapper or anything.

Mrs. Simkewicz sighed. "You're lucky to live so close," she said. "Well, Celie, have a good time. Just call when you want me to come and get you."

I was about to say she didn't have to. Then I figured maybe Mrs. Simkewicz wouldn't like the idea, so I just gave her a trustworthy grin.

When we reached the house, I was telling Celia about the Great Boyd Pearson Gum-Up. Celia laughed in all the right places, so I was in a pretty good mood. We found Mom cleaning up her art stuff. She showed us her sunflower painting, and Celia looked impressed, especially when Mom pulled out the latest batch of flower-design cards.

"They go on sale next week," Mom said. "Mary Ellen just brought over some samples. Pretty neat, huh?"

"They're beautiful!" Celia stood looking at the cards. "Where can I buy them? My mom would love these."

"I'll give you some to take home," Mom promised. "Now, let me get cleaned up and I'll put those burgers on."

She gathered up her brushes. "Now, where did I leave the turpentine?" She glanced around the patio. "Kyle, why don't you run out to the garage and grab that can of paint remover off the tool shelf?"

"Sure, Mom," I said. I turned to Celia. "Sit down anywhere. I'll be back in a sec."

I switched on the light by the garage door, squeezed past Mom's station wagon and Brian's ten-speed bike, and reached for the tool shelf.

Too short by about six inches.

Cursing my height, I went around the car to where Dad stored the firewood. I scrambled on top of the woodpile, and made a lunge for the paint remover.

Just as I grabbed it, the wood shifted under my feet. With a loud clatter I slid onto the oil-stained floor.

"Oh, great!" Firewood lay all over the place. I groaned. Dad would be plenty mad if he came home and found it like this.

I got to my feet, set the paint remover on top of the car, and began gathering up the wood. I'd almost finished making a pile—messy, but at least it was a pile—when I saw them.

Four bottles of Scotch were lined up neatly against the wall. Four shiny brand-new bottles, hidden behind the firewood. All this time they'd been there, when I thought he'd stopped drinking. All this time.

I felt like the biggest dope in the world. Dumber than Arnold Whipple. Gypped. Cheated. A total chump. It didn't matter if he never broke the seals on those bottles. The sneaky part was just as bad.

"Kyle?"

It was Mom. In a flash I remembered that Celia Simkewicz was sitting in my kitchen. Waiting.

I snatched the can of paint remover off the car, sprinted for the door, and shut off the light. "Coming!" I yelled.

Mom looked at me curiously. "What took you so long?"

"Couldn't reach it," I said, handing her the can. "Had to find something to stand on."

I was breathing hard. Mom gave me another look before she poured out some paint remover and set her brushes to soak. I sure hoped she wouldn't make me put the paint remover back. I never wanted to go near that garage again.

CHAPTER
13

Brian got home just as Mom was serving the burgers. He looked from me to Celia, and grinned. "Hey, Squir—" he began. I gave him a warning glare.

Bri laughed. "Squirt some catsup on one of those for me, okay?" he called as he went off to wash his hands.

Mom passed Celia a plate. "Kyle says your family lives in the north end of town."

I watched Celia arrange a paper napkin in her lap. I noticed she did everything in this careful, precise way. I liked noticing stuff about Celia.

She nodded politely. "Yes, on Ledgebrook Road."

Mom paused. "Ledgebrook Road . . . let's see, I've sold a few homes on that street. Do you know the Carsons?"

"They're our next-door neighbors," Celia said. "They play bridge with my parents sometimes."

"Really!" Mom looked thrilled. "Why, I've known the Carsons for years! You should tell your mother to give me a call. I bet we know a lot of people in common." She smiled. "Maybe she can give me a few tips on my bridge game. It's gotten pretty rusty."

While Mom took care of the small talk, I noticed something else about Celia. She was cutting up her hamburger into tiny little pieces. I almost asked what she was doing, but I figured it might be rude. Besides, I kind of liked watching her do it.

Bri came bounding into the room. He sat down across from me and grabbed a hamburger. He took a big bite, and stared at Celia. "So," he said, chewing, "you in Kyle's class?"

She nodded. "We're in Music Appreciation together," she answered, dissecting a piece of sesame-seed bun.

Brian roared with laughter. "I guess you caught the main attraction this morning." He glanced at me. "I heard you stole the show, Squ . . . buddy. Pete's brother told us all about it."

Mom was frowning. "Please show some table manners, Bri. Celia will think you've been raised by wolves."

Brian glanced at the morsels on Celia's plate and lifted one eyebrow. But he grudgingly wiped his mouth and took his elbows off the table.

The bacon burger tasted great, but I wasn't very hungry. I kept glancing at Celia, while Mom talked about her painting and her real estate and what she thought of the local schools. I didn't mind. I was happy to watch Celia, letting the words wash over me.

Brian told a few jokes between helpings. Mom didn't laugh, but Celia and I did. Everything was going off without a hitch. And then Dad showed up.

I didn't even hear the car pull up to the driveway. One

minute Mom was getting up to put some chocolate chip cookies on a plate, and the next minute the front door slammed.

Across the table, Bri tensed. Too late. Dad stood in the door to the kitchen. Or rather, leaned. His eyes were dark and unsmiling.

A funny look passed over Mom's face. It was like a bunch of feelings all colliding together. I watched as she sorted through them: worry, pity, nervousness—until determination won out.

She set the cookies on the table. "Hello, dear," she said. "Working late tonight?"

At least he can't fix himself a drink, I thought. He'd have to go out to the garage to do that.

Then I realized how nuts that was. He didn't need another drink. He was way past the danger zone.

Dad gazed around the table. He looked at Celia and at me. Finally his eyes came to rest on Brian. "You," he said, jabbing a finger in Brian's direction. "Who said you could rifle through my stuff? Don't pretend you don't know what I'm talking about. Because I know what you've been up to."

A sick feeling went through me, as the finger poised in midair. Please, I thought, not tonight, Dad. Not with Celia Simkewicz sitting here. Just—not tonight.

But it was no use. He was glaring at Brian, pointing the old finger of doom at him.

"I'm asking you a question."

"Dad, why don't you go lie down, huh?" Brian said.

"This isn't the time or the place, okay? If you have something to ask me, we can talk about it later. Right now you look like you could use—"

"A hot shower," Mom said firmly. She came around the table and took Dad's briefcase out of his hand. "You're tired, Jim. Brian's right, now isn't the time. Kyle's brought a guest home for dinner and—"

The finger wavered. I held my breath.

After a moment Dad dropped his hand. "I get the picture," he muttered. "I can see how much I count for in this family. . . . Nothing. Nothing at all." He shook his head. Then he turned and walked heavily upstairs.

Silence filled the kitchen like a sick hum. Brian's face was blazing red. I felt Mom touch my shoulder. Then she reached over and squeezed Celia's arm too.

But I couldn't look at Celia. I will never, ever be able to look at Celia Simkewicz again, I thought, as the pain in my stomach throbbed. Not in a million years. Ten million years. Twenty million years.

I kept my eyes glued to the table until they began to feel like peeled grapes. But I didn't care. Now that Celia had met the Stranger, I was sure she would never talk to me again. And I couldn't really blame her.

Then I saw something out of the corner of my eye. A hand reached past me. It lifted a chocolate chip cookie off the plate and set it down at my place.

Slowly I looked up. Celia was smiling at me. As I watched, she reached for another cookie. She didn't break it up into little pieces, either; she bit right into it.

When Celia was on her second cookie, Brian sighed and then grabbed a handful off the plate.

"I'm sorry about what happened, Celia," my brother said, and I was proud of him for having the guts to say it. "Don't hold it against Kyle, okay?"

Celia's head bobbed up and down. "That's okay," she said. She looked around the table. "My dad. . . sometimes he gets in a bad mood too. Especially when he's tired. I mean—it's no big deal."

I felt good when she said that. At least my stomach wasn't throbbing anymore. I took a deep breath. "Listen, can you stay for a little while? We could fool around with the Nintendo. . . ."

Celia smiled. "I'd like to," she said. "But I really have to get home and study. We have that science test tomorrow, remember?"

I didn't remember hearing about any test. But I nodded. "You can use the phone to call your mom . . ."

"I'll drive you home." Brian got to his feet. "No, don't argue. It's a done deal. Mom, you want to give me the keys to the wagon?"

She frowned. "You'll have to move your father's car," she said.

"He didn't drive home. Somebody dropped him off. I saw them slow down in front of the house."

Good, I thought. And for the first time, I pictured Dad trying to drive home from Harrisburg, with his face all red and his eyes blurry and his hands unsteady.

"Kyle, why don't you come along? You can give me

directions." I watched Brian collect the car keys from Mom. Then Celia got up and placed her paper napkin on her chair.

"Thank you very much for dinner," she told Mom. "I hope I can come again sometime."

"Of course, dear. You're welcome anytime." Mom smiled. "Oh, and don't forget your mother's cards."

As Mom handed Celia the box, I remembered the paint remover in the garage, and those four bottles lined up against the wall.

A crummy chill went through me, as something clicked. It was *Brian* who'd taken those bottles off the top shelf in the kitchen, not Dad. Brian, who must have poured the gin and the whiskey and the vodka down the sink and then hidden the bottles in the trash. "I know what you've been up to." The pointing finger. It was Brian, the whole time.

No one said much as we drove across town. All three of us sat in the front seat, Celia in the middle.

When we were almost there, Celia glanced at me. "I hope your team does great, Kyle. We'll all be rooting for you."

For a moment I wondered what she was talking about. Then I remembered: the Knowledge Bowl—passing the math test. With all the fuss over *South Pacific*, I'd managed to forget about it.

"Thanks," I said. "Hey, good luck with the cheerleading. I . . . we'll be rooting for you too."

Celia gave me a sweet, crooked-toothed smile. Then we were in front of her tiny yard, with one raggedy tree in the middle of it. Condo city. Suburbs, in a town that didn't even have an "urb."

"Don't forget your cards," I added, as I slid out of the front seat. She waved them at me and then ran into her house.

Brian and I waited until she got inside. Then we drove back toward town. A few minutes later Bri pulled into the Dairy Dee-Lite. "Hungry, Squirt?"

"I can't believe *you* are. I just watched you eat three chili burgers, with the works. Not to mention half a batch of chocolate chip cookies."

He grinned. "Hey, I'm a growing boy," he said.

"And I'm not?"

The grin vanished. "Aw, Kyle, I didn't mean that."

"I know. But it's true, isn't it? I'm never going to shoot up. That's what Coach Simpson says."

He got out and loped over to the Quik-Order window. I followed. "Coach Simpson's full of it," he told me.

"Possibly. But that doesn't change things, does it? Once a squirt, always a squirt."

Brian ordered a Triple Dee-Lite with nuts and fudge sauce. When the girl handed it to him, he jammed a big spoonful of ice cream in his mouth. Then he pointed the spoon at me.

"That's not true. What're you, thirteen? I know plenty of guys who didn't start growing until they were juniors. Filling out, shooting up, whatever you want to call it.

Frankie Mosconi, he plays for Villanova now? He was still growing when he left for college. God's honest truth."

"Really?"

Brian devoured the sundae in three bites. "Absolutely really. Besides, you don't need to be a giant for track. Next year, give it a shot." He tossed the cup in the trash and let out a healthy belch. Then he shoved his hands in his pockets and looked up at the night sky. "Kyle, can I let you in on a secret?"

I nodded. "I think I know what you're going to say."

Brian smiled. It was a small, knowing smile. Even a little sad. "I don't think so, Squir—sport."

"Is it about Dad?"

"Nope."

I thought about that. If he'd wanted to tell me about emptying the old man's stash, he would have. "So, shoot."

"I'm thinking of joining the Marines. Next year, after I graduate."

He was leaning against the bike stand, one foot looped through the metal bar. He wasn't looking at me. A bright light over the Quik-Order window spread a white mothy pool over our heads, making me squint.

"What about college?" I said, hating how whiny my voice sounded. "Your basketball scholarship?"

Brian's foot hit the ground. He stood and stretched. He looked restless. "I don't want to play basketball for four years," he said. "I don't want to be a college jock. Besides, if I join the Marines, I can still learn something. Electronics or communications, maybe. Plus there's always the GI bill. This way, I can do it on my own."

"Dad's going to kill you, Bri."

"If he doesn't kill himself first," he said quietly.

After a moment, we headed back to the car. I didn't want my brother to join the Marines, maybe end up halfway around the world. But I didn't blame him, either. Being the slam-dunk champion of Wheaton, Pennsylvania might be enough for some guys. But deep down, I always knew it wasn't enough for Bri.

Still, it was a tough ride home. Don't leave me, I wanted to yell. I'm just a kid. I don't know how to fix what's going on at home. I can't do everything myself. And I don't want to end up like Joel Hicks, smiling at everybody and taking it out on the world.

But I didn't say anything. Brian drove through the silent, dark town, staring straight ahead, and neither one of us said a word.

CHAPTER
14

The day before the Knowledge Bowl exam, Rowena and I met for breakfast. The Whipples' kitchen looked like a disaster area. Different-sized Whipples swirled around, getting ready for school. Hands grabbed for the cereal, filled bowls, splashed milk. Mrs. Whipple stood at the counter, making sandwiches and plopping them into six lunch bags. The place was in an uproar.

"Mommmm! Where's my barrette?" "Have you seen where I put my shoes?" "Mom, Soren hit me!"

In the eye of the storm, Arnold sat at the table making disgusting sculptures out of his food. Every once in a while he'd pause to call me a "puke-head." I ignored him. So did Rowena.

Rowena's powers of concentration were stupendous. She told me once that she wanted to become an air traffic controller. I figured her kitchen was a great training ground.

"Here," she said, handing me a box of cereal the size of a stereo speaker. I shook some corn flakes into a bowl. "Now, about the math . . . "

A glob of oatmeal landed in my hair. The Rat gave me an evil smirk. I was about to flip a spoonful of cereal back at him, when Rowena raised her voice above the Whipple uproar. "Kyle, did you study those formulas like I told you to?"

"Well . . . "

She sighed. "You're hopeless, Ky-uhl."

I winced and stared down at my cereal.

"I thought you were going to work at this! What if our team makes the finals, and there's nobody to answer questions about the American Revolution? Huh? Did you ever think about that? I mean, you have a responsibility. To me! To Ms. Loomis! To Wheaton!"

Another glob hit me on the cheek. The Rat was practically wetting his pants with delight.

Without wiping off the oatmeal, I got to my feet and walked around the table. A look of uncertainty crossed the Rat's face. It was replaced by one of sheer terror, as I plunged a spoon into Arnold's stone-cold cereal.

With painstaking care I scooped up a huge mound of oatmeal. As the Rat's mouth froze into a giant O, I pulled open the neck of his chocolate-stained, jam-smeared jersey. Then, like a chef stuffing a turkey, I dumped the oatmeal down the damp cavity of Arnold Whipple's horrible shirt.

Squish! My hand flattened against him, mashing the clammy mess into his round stomach. The revenge of the puke-head was complete.

By the time the Rat's screams erupted, Rowena was

rolling on the floor, choking with laughter. I watched Arnold run squealing off to safety, and savored my victory.

A second later, it was over. Who was I kidding? I thought, as Rowena picked herself off the floor and went back to eating her breakfast. It was easy to feel like a big shot when it came to dumping cereal on a five-year-old.

But unless some miracle happened, by tomorrow I'd be just what my father always told me I was: a zero. A *minus* zero. A worthless screw-up who let down his team, his teacher, the whole town. And there was nothing I could do about it.

The day started out pretty ordinary. Laps in gym, glowers from Boyd—the usual. On my way to class I bumped into Celia. I'd almost decided to talk to her, when her friends came up behind her, cupping their hands over their mouths. I ducked my head and kept walking.

Science. Literary Arts. Music Appreciation.

Mr. Campbell had moved on to marches. If there's one thing I can't stomach right before lunch, it's a pounding military march. It definitely made me miss musicals. Or even a Scottish ballade. Scott and I drew monster mazes while the drums and piccolos and tubas pierced my brain. By the time class was over I felt like a walking musical migraine.

At lunch I quizzed Rowena on her history. Forget about the literature—go for one out of two. She got about half the answers right and seemed pretty pleased.

More classes. More halls. A throbbing piccolo started

up in my head, forcing my feet along. Try not to think about the test, $a + b = z$, so what's z? Left,   right, left, right. Try not to think about your brother marching off to boot camp. The old man was going to go nuts. What did Brian care? I was the one who'd be left to face the music.

The long march ended with the final bell. I thought about going to the last Knowledge Bowl meeting, then decided not to. What was the point? Either I passed or I didn't. Whining about it to Ms. Loomis wasn't going to help.

I picked up my books and headed for the door. It was cold outside, a spooky Halloween-style wind tossing leaves across the softball field. Some kids were kicking a soccer ball off in the distance. I sat down on the dead grass behind the backstop to watch.

I tried to forget about math, about everything. I shoved my chin in my hands and watched the ball sail back and forth, back and forth, the shouts of the soccer players lost in the wind.

"Hey, Kip. Whatcha doing out here, freezing your butt off?"

I looked up. Joel Hicks stood over me, grinning his big, confident grin. I shrugged.

"How come you're not at the meeting?" he asked.

"How come you aren't?"

His grin widened. "I was," he said. "Then I figured I'd better come looking for you. And what do you know? Here you are!"

I got up and brushed the dirt off my pants. "Looking for me? What for?"

Joel laughed. "You sure ask a lot of questions for a knowledge expert," he said. "Hey, I'm just trying to help you, Kip. Just trying to be a pal."

"I don't need any pals," I said. "What I need is a brain transplant." I got up and started walking.

Even though I didn't want him to, Joel fell into step beside me. "It's that math, huh?" he said sympathetically, and in spite of myself, I nodded. He grinned, like he'd just won a bet with himself. "Listen, I told you, Kip. You just have to have the right attitude."

The "Kip" business was starting to get on my nerves. I halted in the middle of the sidewalk and glared at Joel Hicks. "Quit playing games, okay? Just say whatever you have to say. Or get lost."

Joel pretended to take a step back. "Whoa, lighten up, buddy. Looks like you need my help even worse than I thought. Well, lucky for you, your sweating days are over." Before I could say anything, Joel had grabbed my arm and dragged me down an alley, until we were standing under the dead elm tree behind the Bakers' house.

While I was trying to catch my breath, Joel set his book bag on the ground. He glanced up and down the alley. Then he reached in the bag and pulled out some pieces of paper stapled together.

"Here," he said, shoving them at me. "You can thank me later."

I gazed at the top sheet. It looked like the secret codes Scott and I used to make when we were playing Enemy Soldier. Lots of little circles, some of them blacked in, most of them empty. "Thank you? For what?"

"For passing the math test," Joel said. "This is the answer sheet. Get it? You don't have to study. Just memorize it. X marks the spot."

I stared at the piece of paper, while the little black dots danced up and down. X marks the spot . . .

"Come on, Kip," Joel said. "What are you waiting for? I mean, it's no big deal. Everybody does it."

My hand closed around the answer sheet, and my heart began to pound. I could pass math and get on the Knowledge Bowl team, and no one would ever have to know. No one except Joel Hicks, that is. And me.

He was grinning at me, waiting. Then I looked down at what I was holding, and something inside me twisted sharply, like the edge of a knife.

"Where did you get this?" I burst out. "What did you do, Hicks, swipe it? Like that wallet you took at the mall?"

Joel's grin wavered. I felt myself tense, and a weird thought entered my head: Joel is going to hit me. An even stranger one followed: If he does, I'm going to hit him back. It almost made me laugh—all those years of Brian calling me a wimp, and now here it was. The moment of truth.

The strange part was, I didn't even mind. A crummy finish to a crummy day—worrying about Dad and Brian and Rowena, cupped hands over giggles, throbbing piccolos and marching through the halls and a + b = zero. I was ready.

The crib sheet dropped to the ground. My hands

curled at my sides as I waited. Joel's eyes narrowed, and he took a step back. "What's that supposed to mean?" he said loudly.

"What do you think it means?"

"You tell me."

"It means," I said, "that not everyone likes getting expelled for cheating."

That was all it took. Joel was on me like a wounded grizzly bear. All the blood rushed to my face as we toppled over in the dirt. Over and over we rolled. Joel was pummeling me, but I didn't even feel it. I had my hands on his shoulders, trying to push him away. For one moment all I could hear was Joel panting in my face, and a strange grunting noise that sounded like a mad dog. Then I realized it was coming from me.

A second later, it was over. As I tried to get to my feet, my head came up and caught him right in the nose. I heard a dull crack. Then Joel began to moan. Both of us sat up. Blood was pouring down his face.

At the sight of it, all the adrenaline drained out of me. Some fight, I thought, looking at Joel, who was crumpled over, clutching his nose. And in the blue corner, the champion, by technical head butt. Some victory.

I leaned over him. "Let me see." His hands came down and I peered at his nose. It was a mess, but it was still intact. "Put some ice on it," I told him. "You'll be okay. I've caught worse from Boyd Pearson's elbows."

I got up and helped him to his feet. He was making loud snuffling noises, trying to wipe his nose on his sweater, so I gave him my handkerchief. Then I picked up my books and walked down the alley.

All the way home I tried to sort out my thoughts. Maybe, in his own creepy, dishonest way, Joel meant well. Maybe that was his way of being your friend. Stealing you a wallet. Offering you a crib sheet. It was pretty sad.

I let myself in the back door and headed for the kitchen. I was about to make some molasses milk when I caught sight of something in the hall mirror.

A wild-looking kid stared back at me. His hair was a mess; so was the rest of him. His forehead was covered with blood. There was blood all over his clothes, too, along with plenty of dirt.

I stared at myself in amazement. I looked like I'd just walked into a lawnmower. Or been in a fight.

On the other hand, Joel Hicks probably looked even worse.

Joel . . . My guts began to throb where Joel had punched me. I remembered what Dad had said at the ball park. "There goes our future . . . We've got a lot riding on how I impress that man . . . Make his kid feel welcome." What was Dad going to say when he found out I'd given that kid a bloody nose?

I decided I wasn't in a huge hurry to find out. Peeling off my sweater, I hurtled up the stairs.

CHAPTER 15

By the time Mom got home, I'd stuffed my dirty clothes in the hamper, cleaned myself up, and spent an hour staring at Rowena's formulas. It was like looking at the Chinese side of a Chinese menu: You knew it meant something great to someone, but that someone sure wasn't you.

When Mom tapped at my door, I didn't look up.

"Kyle?"

"I'm studying."

"I want to talk to you."

I flashed on everything I might be in trouble for. It wasn't Cindy—she was snoozing under the kitchen table. And the leaves were raked, I'd done that yesterday.

I gave her a big smile. "Sure, Mom. What is it?"

"I just spoke to Mary Ellen Baker. I was dropping off some card designs on my way home. She told me she saw some boys fighting behind her house this afternoon."

My mind formed one thought: uh-oh. "She did?"

"Yes, Kyle, and she said one of them looked like you. I

told her that was impossible, that you don't get into fights, but she was positive it was you."

"She was?"

Mom gave me a searching glance. "Kyle, tell me the truth. Did you get in a fight today?"

I stared down at the math problem. "Kind of," I said.

"Who was it?"

Silence.

"Answer me, Kyle."

"Joel Hicks."

There was a long pause. Then Mom sighed. "Do you want to tell me what happened?"

"Not really," I muttered. I caught a hint of a smile on her face. Then it was gone.

"All right, I'll make this easy for you," she said, plunking her purse down on the rug and folding her arms. "Start talking, young man."

I hesitated. If Joel got in trouble and blamed me, Dad would be the one who paid. *He gets rid of the dead wood,* Joel had said. I couldn't risk it.

"Okay, but you have to promise not to tell Dad."

I waited until I saw her nod. Then I said, "He called me a chicken. But that's not how he put it."

"Oh, Kyle." Mom sank down on my bed. "Don't you know it's better to walk away from something like that?"

I shrugged. "Guess I wasn't in the mood."

She shook her head. "It's just not like you, Kyle." She broke into a half-smile. "Now, Brian—that I could understand. He's battled everything in sight from the time he was a baby. But you . . . Are you sure there isn't something you're not telling me?"

Good old Mom. She could always smell a rat.

"Remember that Knowledge Bowl tournament? How it's a big honor and everything? Well, there's a catch— you've got to take this math test. And there's no way I'm going to pass it, Mom. I've tried, and Rowena's tried, and Ms. Loomis—and nothing helps. I'm doomed!"

Mom rested her cheek on her hand and looked at me. For one scary second I wondered if she knew the real story behind the fight with Joel. It was that kind of look.

Then she patted the bed. "Come here," she said.

I walked over and sat down.

"Remember how I said your dad would help you if you asked him? Well, he will. Hush," she said, when I started to protest. "Now, I know things haven't been one hundred percent perfect around here. But when it matters, your dad is there for you. I promise you, Kyle. All you have to do is ask."

She made it sound so simple.

I waited until dinner was over. Dad was in the living room, going over some papers. I gathered up the sample questions and what little guts I had and approached him.

"Dad? Got a minute?"

He put the papers down and rubbed his eyes. "Sure, son. What is it?"

"It's . . . about math. I'm having a little trouble figuring out these problems. Mom said maybe you could give me some pointers."

He smiled. It was a tired smile, but at least it didn't make me want to run out of the room. "She did, huh? Well, let's have a look."

He made room for me on the couch, and I showed him the problems. Dad tapped his nose and said "hmm" a couple of times. Then he grabbed his calculator and went through each problem, showing me how it was done.

Math sure is slippery stuff. Whenever I watch other people do it, I almost get it. But when it's my turn, all those signs and directions and footholds disappear.

Watching Dad, I had a feeling the same thing was going to happen, but I thanked him anyway. "You're really good at this stuff," I added. "Were you always?"

"When I was your age, you mean?" He grinned and shook his head. "It takes practice, just like anything else. Once you get to high school, you'll get the hang of it."

"I just hope I get the hang of it by tomorrow."

"Keep plugging away, Kyle. You've got the brains in this family. I know you can do it." He smiled and reached for his stack of papers.

I folded up the practice sheet. "Looks like you've got a lot of work to do," I said, staring at the pile of folders on the couch.

"There's a district meeting coming up tomorrow. I have to give a presentation on how our branch is doing."

"A big deal, huh, Dad?"

"Make or break." He smiled again, but he didn't look happy. "Mr. Hicks expects a full report on every account. Every account!" He groaned and shook his head. "And the figures better add up. Or I'm going to be in hot water."

"I guess that's what calculators are for, right?" I said.

Dad was flipping through his spreadsheets. "Well, you see, there's different ways of adding. The trouble starts when the calculator says something you don't want it to. So then you have to start over until the numbers come out looking a little better."

He laughed at my expression. "Don't worry, Kyle. You'll figure it out the first time you have to do your own income tax return."

Maybe so, but I still felt confused. How was I supposed to pass this math test when someone as smart as my dad couldn't make things add up? Besides, a calculator was just a machine, wasn't it? How could numbers add up differently?

Then I looked down at the spreadsheet, and I knew why he'd laughed. Dad's numbers weren't just $a + b = x$. They stood for dollars and cents. Dad meant he had to make it look like his branch had made a lot of money. Even if it hadn't.

But I didn't say anything. I stuck the practice sheet in my pocket and headed for the kitchen. Maybe Joel was right after all, I thought. Everybody did it.

I grabbed a glass of milk and drank it down in one gulp. Then I went upstairs to go through the math problems one more time. But my heart wasn't in it. I felt stupid and tired and about a hundred years old. My cheek slipped down on the workbook, and I shut my eyes.

I was dreaming I was on a pirate ship. The pirates had Celia tied up, and I was trying to save her. A fierce battle raged on deck. As the action swirled around me, I fought my way over to Celia, my sword drawn.

A big pudgy pirate with an eye patch stood in my path: Black Boyd. I slashed my sword at him, and he yelped and dove away. I *had* to save Celia. But the pirates kept coming. One with a peg leg looked an awful lot like Coach Simpson. Heartlessly, I tossed him overboard.

But it was no use. There were too many pirates. Celia began to cry as the sounds of the battle grew louder and louder.

I lifted my head from the workbook. There was a battle going on, all right, but it was coming from downstairs. Dad and Brian were yelling at each other.

"Don't lie to me," I heard Dad say. "I talked to your coach today. He said you've already missed two appointments with college recruiters."

"And I'm saying this has nothing to do with you, Dad! I don't need you checking up on me."

"I wasn't checking up on anyone. I was in the hardware store. Don Peters comes up to me and says, what's going on with your kid, Jim? Can't seem to make him talk to any recruiters. Two top schools ready to sign, he says, and you're nowhere to be found. He thinks it's drugs. I tell him that's baloney. Not *my* kid!" Dad's voice shook. "No way!"

I sat still, trying not to listen. But it didn't work. After a moment I went to the top of the stairs and looked down.

Dad and Bri were circling each other in the middle of the living room. Mom sat on the couch, her head down.

"I'm not on drugs, Dad." Bri's voice was impatient. "And I did talk to a recruiter."

There was a pause. Then Dad said, "You did?"

"But not for basketball. It was a Marine recruiter who came to school on career day. I'm thinking of joining up."

A frozen silence filled the room. I held my breath.

Finally Mom spoke up. "When, Brian?"

"Next June, right after graduation."

Dad began to argue. But Brian interrupted. "I'll be eighteen, Dad. I've made up my mind. I'm not ready to go to college and be someone's basketball star. Maybe when I get out. But not right now. I want to do this *my* way."

"And just what are you trying to prove with this stunt?" Dad's tone was low and angry. "That you're a big man? That you can stand on your own feet? You know what life holds for guys who don't have a college education, Mr. Big Shot?"

"But I will have an education," Brian said, and his voice sounded worn thin. "I'll get training in the Corps, and then I can go on to school when I finish. And I'm not trying to prove anything to anybody. Except maybe to myself."

Dad shook his head. "You're throwing your life away, Brian."

"You ought to know, Dad," Brian shot back.

"You're pretty much the expert on that!"

They say that when animals sense danger, they flee. I guess with me, it's just the opposite. As the voices downstairs rose, I started for the stairs.

Mom saw me first. She shook her head, like she didn't want me to be part of what was going on. Then Dad turned around and saw me too.

"Kyle," he said. His face seemed to sag, and he blinked a couple of times.

Bri looked up. "It's okay, Squirt," he said. "I was just telling Mom and Dad about my plans. Guess I didn't do such a great job."

"You leave your brother out of this," Dad growled. "Kyle, this has nothing to do with you. Go to your room."

"But Dad—"

"Now."

I decided not to argue. I took a few steps up the stairs.

After a moment, Dad walked over to the couch and gathered up his papers. "At least I've got one smart kid," he said, almost under his breath. "One son who isn't going to blow his whole future."

He picked up the files and brushed past me. The door to his study slammed.

No one moved for a second.

Then Mom got up and walked over to Brian. "I'm awfully proud of you, kid," she told him and she gave him a big hug.

"What about Dad?" Brian asked.

"Don't you worry about Dad. Just leave him alone— he'll get used to the idea." Mom paused. "Now, wasn't there some ice cream you were going to get at the store for me?"

Brian glanced at the dark windows. "Now, Mom?"

"Yes, now. You can take the station wagon." She went to the peg by the phone where she kept the car keys. Looking puzzled, Brian took the keys and headed for the door.

When he was gone, Mom turned to me. "I think they both needed a chance to catch their breath, don't you? And now, if you're such a smart kid, how about beating your old mom at a game of cribbage?"

The smart kid got beat five games in a row. About an hour later, Brian came back with a quart of strawberry ice cream. We all had some before bed. Except for Dad, that is. He was still up in his study, crunching numbers.

Maybe it was those two helpings of ice cream. Maybe it was the math test tomorrow. But when I got to bed, I couldn't sleep. As I wrestled with the sheets, I noticed a faint sound coming through the wall: the tapping of calculator keys.

I lay awake a long time, listening to the town of Wheaton get quiet, until it was so late it was almost early, and the crows began to quarrel in the tops of the trees. Even so, the tapping never stopped.

CHAPTER
16

The Knowledge Bowl test was scheduled for right after school.

At lunch I stared at the practice problems, in case any answers decided to stick in my head. When I looked up, I saw Joel crossing the cafeteria. His nose looked pretty swollen; otherwise he seemed like his old self. Except that when he saw me looking at him, he turned and walked to the other side of the room.

All day the ball of dread grew in my stomach, until it was the size of a cantaloupe. Dad's voice kept ringing in my head. "At least I've got one smart kid," he'd said.

One smart kid. Over and over, like the bell of doom, until this other thought took over: I'm going to ace this test if it kills me.

On my way to the exam room, I saw Celia Simkewicz. She was carrying her cheerleader uniform over her arm, heading for practice.

She stopped and smiled at me. "Hi, Kyle. How come you're still here? Did someone make you stay after?"

"Nope," I said. "They're giving the test for the Knowledge Bowl today. To see who gets on the team."

133

Celia's eyes widened. "Poor you," she said. "Taking a test when you don't even have to."

"Yeah," I said, grinning a little. "Poor me."

"How do you think you'll do?" she asked. "On the test?"

"I'm not sure. Okay, I hope."

Celia's mouth opened into a big O, and her eyelashes fluttered with concern. Right then I decided that I liked Celia Simkewicz better than anyone in the whole world.

"Oh, I hope so too, Kyle!" she said.

Shifting her uniform to the crook of her arm, she reached up and undid one of her barrettes, so that the blond hair spilled down over her face. "Here," she said, handing it to me. "For luck."

The barrette was made out of some kind of shiny plastic. It had little glitters all over it, and it was still warm from her hair. My fingers closed around it.

"I'll be looking for you on the team," she said.

"Thanks, Celia," I told her. "I'll give it my best shot."

Then I shoved the barrette in my pocket and hurried down the hall to meet Rowena.

A green test booklet lay on each desk as the team filed into the room. Ms. Loomis sat at the front, a reassuring smile on her face.

"Take a seat," she told us. "Leave at least one space between you and your neighbor. And no X-ray vision, please."

That brought a strained chuckle.

"You have one hour to complete all four sections of the

test. When you finish one, go on to the next. Once you're done, you may bring your answer sheet up to me and then leave."

Rowena raised her hand. "When do we find out whether or not we passed?" she asked.

"As soon as I do," Ms. Loomis answered cheerfully. "I'll start checking your answer sheets once they're all turned in," she added, as we all groaned. "Now, relax. I know everyone is going to do just fine!"

I waited until she reached my desk and felt her pat me on the shoulder. Then I picked up the sharpened pencil and opened the booklet.

The literature test was a breeze. History was a joke. Social studies had a few toughies, but I'd watched enough world news to make a decent stab at them.

Then I looked at the first math question. The cantaloupe in my stomach grew to the size of a watermelon.

"A kite string makes an angle of 50° with level ground. If the string is 65 feet long, how high is the kite above ground?"

They might as well have asked me to explain the mysteries of the universe. I pictured myself at the end of that kite string, soaring above the school, while I waited for the ground to rush up and swallow me.

I could hear the scratching of pencils as everyone filled in their circles. I pictured Joel scanning the pattern he'd memorized, then whizzing through the answers. Across the room, Rowena worked away, all those formulas and theorems tucked away inside her head.

My own head was as empty as Main Street on a Sunday afternoon. My heart began to bang in panic. I tried to remember what Dad had shown me, but my mind felt like a block of cement. If there was an answer buried in there, it would take a stick of dynamite to blast it out.

Even so, I tried. "When the angle of the sun is 59°, a building casts a shadow 85 feet long. How high is the building?"

The building is very, very high, I thought blankly. I didn't care how tall the building was. I just wanted to jump off it.

One by one, kids finished and dropped their answer sheets on Ms. Loomis's desk. I squinted at the questions, trying out one answer after another. The last problem had something to do with five guys trading green and yellow tickets for red and blue ones. None of it made any sense. My head began to ache.

I glanced around the room. Rowena sat off to the side, double-checking her answers. A girl named Myra Babbitt was hunched so far over her test booklet, she was practically lying on top of it. And then there was me. Everyone else had gone.

Sorry, Dad, I thought. Even a screw-up knows when he's licked. With a sigh, I colored in one of the circles at random, and closed the book on my future.

Off in the distance a buzzer sounded. Ms. Loomis looked up from her desk. Rowena had left, and now the only people sitting there were me and Myra, the pokiest person at Wheaton Junior High. Half the time she never made it to school on time. But even old Myra managed to beat the clock. I watched her get up and hand in her test.

When the door closed behind her, Ms. Loomis looked at me and smiled. "I'm afraid your time's up, Kyle," she called. I just sat there, Celia's barrette poking me in the hip.

"Kyle? Would you bring me your test, please?"

It seemed to take ten minutes to walk to the front of the room. "Here," I said, putting the booklet on top of the pile. "For what it's worth," I added.

"Don't talk like that," Ms. Loomis said. She frowned. "Whatever happens, you tried your best. And that's all that anyone can ask."

"I guess."

Ms. Loomis sat there studying me with her kind brown eyes. "Kyle? Is there something you need to talk about?"

"No," I said. Then why was I standing there like an idiot? "It's just that—"

I never got a chance to explain what it was. The door to the exam room flew open, and Cheryl Marks, who worked in the principal's office, poked her head in the room. Her face was red, and I could tell she'd been running.

"Ms. Loomis!" she squealed, very official and important. "You're wanted on the phone right away. It's urrrgent!"

Ms. Loomis gave me a quick glance. "Just sit tight, Kyle. I'll be right back. My goodness, Cheryl, calm down. I'm coming." I stood there with my mouth open while she followed Cheryl out the door. I could hear the rat-a-tat of their shoes as they disappeared down the hall.

Silence filled the room. I gazed at the floor, waiting for Ms. Loomis to come back. I wasn't sure what I'd meant to say. Maybe just apologize for screwing up the team's chances. Explain there was a rutabaga in my head where the math part was supposed to be. Promise Ms. Loomis that I would never, ever try out for anything again, so long as I lived.

After a while, I got bored. I looked out the window. I peered up at the clock. I sat down and then stood up again. Finally my eyes drifted down to the answer sheets on Ms. Loomis's desk.

I tried to tell myself I hadn't really blown it. After all, Rowena was the only math ace in the group, if you didn't count Joel. I chewed my lip and thought about it. At least I finished; that must count for something. After a moment, I decided to see if old Myra Babbitt had managed to answer all the questions, too.

I lifted my answer sheet and peeked at Myra's. Sure enough, she'd finished. That made me feel even worse. Dad wouldn't call me his smart kid if he knew poky Babbitt had done just as well. Maybe better.

And then, underneath Myra's answer sheet, I caught sight of Rowena's. Just the corner of it, her name printed across the top. But the minute I saw it, a sick plan began to form in my head.

I stood there fighting it. Should I or shouldn't I? I shouldn't because it was wrong, I told myself. Just as wrong as Joel Hicks's crib sheet. Just as bad.

But Joel wasn't doing it for a worthy cause. Joel didn't

care about anybody but himself. If the team ever made it to Harrisburg, Joel Hicks would be worthless.

I, on the other hand, could at least contribute something.

Besides, my parents were counting on me. "Make us proud," they always said. Not "disappoint us" or "let us down," but "make us proud." Proud meant winning stuff. Showing people you had what it takes.

I pulled out the barrette and watched it sparkle in the light. Celia would be at the assembly when the new computer system was awarded to Wheaton Junior High. All because of me. Celia waving her pom-poms, worship in her eyes. Just like in a musical.

Then I pictured Rowena. We were best friends: she'd do anything for me. I could explain later, remind her how we were a team, helping each other when it counted.

Anyway, like Joel said—everybody did it. No big deal. When the numbers came out wrong, you just had to start over until they came out right.

I pulled Rowena's answer sheet out of the pile and glanced at the last section. Picking up a pencil, I erased my wild guesses and filled in the right answers. With a thudding heart, I placed the tests back in the pile.

Thirty seconds later, the door to the room opened and Ms. Loomis walked in. Right then, my conscience zoomed back from wherever it had gone. I felt lower than a toadstool. I felt lousy.

But it was too late. It was done.

Then I noticed her face was white and sort of grim-looking. A crazy alarm went off in my head, and I thought, what if she *saw* me? What if she'd been standing there the whole time!

A cold sweat broke out all over me. Maybe this was some secret honesty test, and now I'd be led away to the principal's office to be punished, called a cheater, expelled from school.

Instead, Ms. Loomis walked over and put her hand on my shoulder. "Kyle?" she said in this low, scary voice that's supposed to make you feel calm, but doesn't. "Your mother's coming to take you to the hospital. I'm afraid there's been an accident."

"An—an accident?" For some reason, all I could picture was Brian on his bike, thrown to the side of the road, his body mangled and broken.

A weird shiver went through me. Brian was hurt, and I was the cause of it. I'd just done something bad, and now my family would have to be punished. It was as simple as that.

"Is it my . . . brother?" I asked, half choking as the fear welled up in my throat.

Ms. Loomis shook her head, and her brown eyes got very big and very sad. I felt her hand tighten on my shoulder.

"No, Kyle," she said. "It's your dad."

CHAPTER
17

Mom and I didn't talk much on the way to the hospital.

"Is Dad all right?" I asked as soon as I got in the car.

I could see the worry in her eyes, but she didn't let on. "The patrolman said it was just a fender-bender. You know how people drive these days. Your dad must have been in too big a hurry and didn't watch where he was going."

I nodded. "Sure, Mom."

As we turned onto the highway, I stared at the bare trees and the stubble on the frozen fields. But all I could see was the way Dad's eyes looked when he came home late, and the way he stumbled when he walked, and how his hands shook.

For the rest of the ride, I kept my eyes on the traffic and tried not to think.

When we reached the hospital, Bri was waiting at the entrance. "Coach told me," he said. "How is he?"

"He's in the emergency room," was all Mom said. The automatic doors swished open, and we walked down a green hall.

A highway patrolman stood at the admitting counter,

filling out some forms. There was another hall with rooms on each side. A nurse pointed us to the second door on the left.

Dad was sitting up on the examining table. Except for a cut on his forehead, he didn't look too bad. He had his shirt off, and he was talking to a nurse who was bandaging his rib cage.

When he saw us standing at the door, his face tightened and he bit his lip.

"Am I hurting you, Mr. Maxwell?" the nurse asked.

"No, no," Dad said. "You're doing a fine job."

She smiled and taped the end of the bandage under his arm. "There," she said. "You can see your family now." With another smile she left, closing the door behind her.

Mom took a few steps toward Dad. "Jim—"

"Just some bruised ribs." Dad reached for his shirt. Then he winced and sat back. "Hurts a little when I take a deep breath. Reminds me of my old football playing days." He tried to smile, but it wasn't much of one.

Mom picked up the shirt and helped him into it. Brian was leaning against the door. After a moment, he shoved his hands in his pockets and looked at Dad. "So," he said. "What happened?"

I saw Dad stiffen. Mom did too, and she stopped fussing with the shirt. All three of us waited.

"It was a rough meeting," Dad said after a moment. "Chuck Peters gave his report, and Hicks just ripped it to shreds. By the time it was my turn, everyone was pretty wound up. I did the best I could. But it was no use."

He was hunched forward, staring into space. I thought of the stack of files, the calculator keys tapping into the night. For a moment I almost felt sorry for him.

"When we broke for lunch, I knew it wasn't going to fly. Nobody said anything, but I just had that sick feeling in my gut. Anyway—I didn't go back to the meeting. I went to a bar instead. I don't remember what I was thinking. Just sort of crazy, I guess. Didn't want to think."

Mom put her hand on his shoulder. But Dad didn't seem to notice. He looked wound up, intent on what he was saying.

"I must have left around two. I knew I'd had too much, but I thought I could make it home. Didn't even see the lady in that other car. The trooper who stopped said I was all over the road. He'd been following me for half a mile, and I didn't even know it." Dad shook his head, like he was trying to wake up from a bad dream, or make sense of something.

There was silence for a moment. Then someone knocked on the door. It was the nurse. "Mr. Maxwell, if you're ready, the officer wants to see you now."

Dad nodded and grasped Mom's hand. I watched her help him down from the table.

Then she turned to Brian. "We might be a while. Why don't you guys wait for us at home?" She fished in her purse. "Here's the keys to the wagon. Oh, and stop by the garage and check on the Taurus, okay?"

Bri pocketed the car keys. I saw him glance at Dad.

He was turned away from us, his back stiff and straight.

His eyes were trained on the floor, like he didn't want any-one looking at him.

I hated seeing him like that, looking so ashamed. I wanted to say something, to tell him everything would be okay.

Then I looked down the hall, where the patrolman was waiting at the front desk. I saw the scared look on Mom's face. I thought of what Dad had done, how he could have killed someone, driving like that, and it made me feel sick.

I stared at Dad's stiff back. What if the kids at school found out what happened? What if he had to go to jail? Pearson would really have a field day then. I pictured Ms. Loomis, the pity in her eyes. All of a sudden I didn't feel sorry for Dad anymore. I didn't even want to look at him.

I punched Bri on the shoulder. "Come on," I said. "Let's go home."

On the way, we stopped at the Texaco station and checked out Dad's car. The front end was demolished.

"He sure was lucky," the mechanic said. "So was the lady he rear-ended. What was he, asleep at the wheel?"

"Sort of," I said. The guy shook his head and went back to work on another car.

Brian was examining one of the crumpled fenders. I walked over and stood next to the car.

"Are you mad at Dad?" I asked.

"Maybe." He ran his hand over the scratched paint job. "Are you?"

I shrugged. "But . . . I guess it's good this happened.

Right, Bri? I mean, maybe Dad's learned the hard way."

"Learned what?" Bri's blue eyes were trained on me. Being the slam-dunk king of Wheaton, my brother has the eyes of a hawk. It was like being pinned in a pair of high beams.

I swallowed. "That he's a problem drinker," I said finally. "That he can't have just one beer or one vodka or one anything. That bad things happen when he does."

Brian straightened up from the wrecked car. "You know what? Maybe it *is* good this happened." And he clapped me on the back and grinned, like I was the one who had learned something.

"Come on, genius," he said. "Let's get you home so you can hit the books. Because the way I hear it, Wheaton's going to need you, if they want to cream those chumps at the Brain Drain."

Bam! It all came back, then: erasing the answers, copying Rowena's, sticking the test back in the pile.

"Sure," I muttered. "Let's go."

But as I followed Bri out of the garage, my guts felt as twisted as the fenders on Dad's car.

When we got home, Brian went outside to shoot some baskets. I sat at the kitchen table and tried to look at my homework, but it was tough to concentrate.

I reached in the back of my notebook for my social studies assignment. Instead, I pulled out the practice sheet from Music Appreciation: the words to "Bali Ha'i."

I stared at the lyrics. Dad said the song was about a special place where people could go to escape their problems. I remembered wondering what he was talking about. Now I understood, all right. If there was a place like Bali Ha'i—or even just a slab of rock in the middle of the ocean—I'd definitely be on the next boat.

Instead, I put away my books and turned on a ball game.

Around six-thirty Mom called and said they were meeting with a lawyer and not to wait up. Bri went out and got some tacos. We ate them in front of the TV.

I was almost asleep when I felt Mom lean over the bed and kiss me on the cheek. "Hi," I said. "What happened? Did Dad get arrested?"

"We'll talk about it tomorrow. Did you guys eat?"

"Yeah, we had some tacos. So what did the lawyer say?"

Mom smiled. "I think we could all use a good night's sleep."

"Sure, Mom."

"And Kyle? Thanks for being my good kid. I don't know what I'd do without you." And she gave me another quick kiss.

The good kid made it to school one minute ahead of the bell. Joel Hicks was waiting by my locker when I got there.

"Did you hear the news?" he asked.

I tried to stay cool. "What? Did Pearson try to eat a sixth-grader and choke to death?" I reached past him and shoved my books in the locker.

"Ms. Loomis posted the list for the Knowledge Bowl team. It's you, me, Whipple, and Babbitt."

"Myra? You're kidding me!" I groaned, to cover the punch from the battering ram that had suddenly taken over my stomach. "By the time she decides to press the buzzer, the whole thing will be over!"

Joel smiled. "So," he said, "looks like you didn't need my help with that math after all." Then his voice dropped. "Listen, no hard feelings, right? I mean, we're still friends, aren't we, Kip?"

Behind the big grin, Joel looked nervous. I wondered if the was worried that I'd turn him in. I felt like telling him he didn't have to be. As of yesterday, we were in the same boat. And it wasn't heading for Bali Ha'i.

I punched him on the arm. "Sure thing, Joel," I said. "No problem."

During activities period, Ms. Loomis made it official. She had the four of us stand up while the other kids gave us a round of applause. Rowena kept squealing in my ear and squeezing my hand until the knuckles popped.

"I knew you could do it, Kyle," she yelled. "If you just believed in yourself. And I was right. Harrisburg, here we come!"

The battering ram gave me a good one right in the gut.

CHAPTER 18

After the meeting I told Rowena about Dad's accident. "I wanted you to hear it from me," I finished. "In case it got around school or anything."

She was quiet for a moment, like she was thinking hard. "Don't worry," she said. "I won't tell. And if anybody says anything, I'll make 'em wish they hadn't!"

I winced. "That's okay, Rowena. I can take care of myself."

"I know," Rowena said. "But I'm still glad you told me. I mean, we're friends, right? So friends can tell each other anything."

The rest of the way home, I didn't say a word.

When we reached her house, Rowena paused. "Don't forget to study," she said. "The semi-finals are only two weeks away."

"I won't." With a wave, I headed across the street and turned up our driveway.

Brian was in the garage, working on the station wagon. He straightened up when he saw me.

"Figured I'd get Mom's car in shape while the Taurus

is being fixed," he explained. "She sure left it a mess." He tossed me a bag of trash.

"How come you're not at practice?"

"Told Coach I needed some time off. He's so mad at me for not going to Villanova, he didn't argue."

I took the trash out to the garbage pail. On my way back I checked behind the stack of firewood. Sure enough, the bottles were still there.

"So that's where he kept them." Brian stood behind me, looking down at the woodpile.

"You couldn't find all his hiding places. No one could."

"Hey, it was worth a try." He scratched his head. "Should have figured it out, though. The way he'd buy all that wood, whether we needed it or not . . ."

We stood there looking at the bottles. "Do you think he'll be okay?" I asked after a moment. "That now he'll stop drinking?"

Brian shrugged. "It's up to Dad. We didn't make him start drinking. So we sure can't make him stop."

"No," I said slowly. "I guess not."

Brian turned back to the station wagon. He reached for the vacuum cleaner, and then paused. "Saw you coming up the street with Whipple," he remarked. "You guys still cramming for that knowledge thing?"

"Knowledge thing?"

"C'mon, you know. The Brain Drain. Do you think you bagged a spot on the team?"

"Yeah," I said. "I did."

A big smile crossed Bri's face, and he clapped me on

the back. "Hey, way to go, buddy. You must be really pumped!"

"Yeah. I mean, I guess so."

Brian peered at me. "What's wrong, Squirt?" he asked. "Worried about Mom and Dad?"

"Nah . . ."

Bri leaned against the station wagon and sighed. "Listen, Kyle. You can tell me to go take a hike. But if you're just doing this for them, you're going to be sorry."

"What do you mean?"

"I mean, I know how it is. Don't get me wrong," he added. "I like basketball. But the trophies and the championships and the titles? That was all Dad's idea, not mine."

Then he smiled. "Hey, I think it's great you're a brain, I really do. Just don't do it for Dad, or the Rowena Monster, or some teacher. They don't have to live inside your skin. You do."

I nodded. After a moment he flipped me a can of soda out of the cooler. "Did I tell you? Pete Kenyon's selling me his car."

I tossed the can back at him. "No way! The Celica? Yellow, with a racing stripe?"

Brian grinned. "He says the transmission's shot, but it's not as bad as he thinks. I'm getting a steal."

He rubbed his chin, like he was making this big decision. "Sooo, guess it's time to say adios to the old bike."

"Adios?"

"Figured I might donate it to a worthy cause. There's

probably some orphan who'd like to ride it."

"Bri—"

He grinned. "On second thought, I guess it has 'Squirt' written all over it. That is, if you can reach the pedals."

When I finished pounding him, I let out a whoop old Fenwick the pigeon could hear clear out in his cage. "Your bike! I can't believe it! You hardly ever let me ride it!"

"Hey, just being practical here. I'd look pretty stupid reporting for boot camp on a ten-speed, wouldn't I?"

I didn't bother to argue. I was already wheeling the bike out of the garage to admire the thin tires and the cool gears.

After dinner, I rode around the neighborhood on my new ten-speed. I tried not to think about stuff, just let the wind rush past my face, focus on the smooth pumping of the pedals, let everything fall away.

It didn't work. I kept hearing Brian telling me not to do stuff for Dad or Mom or Rowena—to do it for myself.

The only problem was—which stuff?

I looked at my new bike. It didn't have a clue. With a sigh, I put it back in the garage and went inside to study.

Right before lunch Rowena came rushing up.

"Ms. Loomis wants to see you right away." She gave me an encouraging poke. "I bet it's good news!"

I almost told her that was a lousy bet. Instead I gave Rowena a phony smile and headed off down the hall to see Ms. Loomis.

When I got there, she was taking a lunch sack out of her drawer. She smiled when she saw me. "Hi, Kyle. Have a seat."

"No, that's okay." My voice gave a loud squeak, but Ms. Loomis didn't seem to notice.

She began to unwrap her sandwich. "How's your dad?" she asked.

I checked her face in case she'd heard anything. "He's going to be okay," I said. "Just some bruised ribs and stuff."

"Oh, Kyle, that's great." Ms. Loomis paused. "But that isn't what I wanted to talk to you about."

"It isn't?"

Her grin widened. "Kyle, how would you like to be the captain of our Knowledge Bowl team?"

The squeak got worse. "Me?"

"Your test scores were great. Best of the whole team. I knew all that studying would pay off." Her brown eyes sparkled. "Well, how about it? Can you take us all the way to Harrisburg?"

I tried to smile back, but all kinds of stuff began running through my head.

Mostly it came down to one thing: Ms. Loomis was my favorite teacher. She believed in me. There was no way I could tell her I'd cheated on the test. No way on earth.

I started to nod.

And then, as I looked at Ms. Loomis, a weird thing happened. I couldn't move my head. The more I tried to nod, the stiffer my neck got.

The clock ticked in the quiet room. It sounded louder than a freight train. Ms. Loomis was staring at me, waiting. I could feel my face getting hot. I took a long, shaky breath.

"I can't be captain of the team," I said. "I—I copied Rowena's answer sheet. When you were out of the room." My voice sounded rusty, like a broken hinge. "I know it was wrong. But I didn't want to let you down. Or the team . . ."

"Kyle, look at me."

Reluctantly I raised my eyes.

"I know you had good intentions. And I'm sure it's tempting, when you hear how everybody does it. But cheating is still wrong, even if a million people do it. And it doesn't make you feel very good inside, does it?"

"No," I mumbled.

"But I'm not sure you understand who you hurt the most."

It wasn't a multiple choice question. I shook my head.

"How about Rowena Whipple?"

"But she wanted me to make the team," I said. It sounded pretty lame, even to me. "I figured she'd be sore if I didn't."

Ms. Loomis didn't blink. "Do you know what friendship is, Kyle? It's trust. And that's what you betrayed." She shook her head. "Once a person's trust is gone, it's pretty hard to win it back. I can't say I envy you."

She gave me a long look. Finally, she picked up her sandwich again. "The principal has set up a program for ethics violators," she said. "You'll be required to work on a school beautification project. Painting the building, planting shrubs, playground duty. In your case, I think a month will suffice. That's every day, after school. Think you can handle it?"

It seemed like a pretty light sentence. "That's all?"

"No, not quite. Your parents will have to be told. And I'm sorry, Kyle, but I'm suspending you from the team. No cheating allowed, not even with good intentions. Those are the rules."

Did the rules include Joel? I thought about it. I would have loved to rat on him. But Joel Hicks didn't live in my skin either. He could take his own lumps.

I started for the door.

Then I turned back. "Can I ask a favor?"

Ms. Loomis nodded.

"I'd like to nominate Rowena for captain of the team."

"I'll give it serious consideration." She tapped her chin for a moment. "For what it's worth, I think it takes guts to admit when you've done wrong. To come forward and accept the blame. It takes a special kind of person, Kyle."

She smiled. "When I talk to your mom, I'll tell her that."

I gulped. "Yes, Ms. Loomis."

I decided to clear out before she got any more good ideas. Still, I felt better than I had in a long time. I was sick of storing up secrets. No more secrets, no more lies.

That's what I'd tell Rowena, I decided, when I explained why I was off the team. Like she said, we were friends. And friends could tell each other anything.

I pushed open the door and took a step into the hall. Then I stopped.

Rowena stood next to the door, a stricken expression on her face.

For one long, horrible moment we stared at each other. Then she turned and raced off down the hall, practically bumping into the walls to get away from me.

No more secrets, no more lies. It didn't matter now.

Rowena the snoop had heard every word.

CHAPTER 19

I lined up my third stack of Oreos and stared at them.

Ten was a lot of Oreos, even for someone who was trying to shoot up. Then I remembered that Mom and Dad were over at school, and that Ms. Loomis was talking to them at this very moment.

Anything was better than thinking about that. I stuffed two Oreos down the hatch.

By the time Mom and Dad came home, the counter was covered with black crumbs, and my stomach was a mess. Mom glanced at the crumbs and then at the bag of cookies. "Dinner's in an hour, Kyle," she said.

Then she touched Dad's arm. "I'm going to the store for a few things. I'll be back in a little while."

When she was gone, Dad sat down at the counter. I pretended to clean up some crumbs so I wouldn't have to look at him.

Dad cleared his throat once or twice, and leaned forward.

"Your teacher told us what happened," he said.

"Yeah, I figured."

"She says you cheated because you thought you had to. That otherwise you'd let everybody down. Is that true?"

"I shouldn't have done it, Dad. I know it was wrong."

He squinted at me. "Did you think winning was more important than playing fair? Is that what I taught you, Kyle?"

"You always told us to stay one step ahead of the competition. To make sure we were the best at whatever we did."

"Well, you just took a crooked step, Kyle. And those don't count. Not in my book."

"Dad, I—"

"No excuses, Kyle."

He got up and began to pace around the kitchen. I braced myself. In another minute he'd go into his Salesman of the Year routine, telling me how Maxwells were winners, and winners don't cheat.

Finally Dad stopped pacing. He stuck his hands in his pockets and gave me a long look.

"Kyle, I want to talk about what happened. The day I went to the hospital."

"I know what happened," I said stiffly. "You got in an accident—"

"Yes," Dad said, "and it wasn't the first time."

I stared at him. Not the first time?

"Does that mean you're going to jail?" I asked.

He shook his head. "No. But I will have to complete an alcohol program."

"What's that?"

"It's like a class. They teach people about drinking and driving, and a lot of other stuff."

"What kind of stuff?"

"Talking, mostly. About how to handle problems. That when something's wrong, it's okay to ask for help. To tell people what's going on, instead of . . . taking a drink."

Dad paused. "I've never been good at that, Kyle. Talking about stuff, I mean. So don't expect any miracles, okay? At least, not for a while."

"I won't," I said.

We were both quiet. Dad was staring at the floor, rocking back and forth on his heels. Right then, he didn't look like the Chair-Man of the Bored, the fastest-talking sales rep in central Pennsylvania, the guy who was always one step ahead of the competition.

All my life, Dad had talked about getting into the winner's circle, about being the best. Maybe, I thought, part of being a winner was what you did to get there. How you felt about yourself, whether you won or lost.

I thought about Joel and his "positive attitude." Some attitude. Dad was right, there weren't any miracles. No quick fixes, no easy outs. Sure, you could cheat, or take a drink—but you didn't end up liking yourself much. And what kind of prize was that?

"Hey, Dad?"

His head came up. "Hmm?"

"What you said just now, about telling people what's going on?"

He nodded.

"How would you feel if . . . if we made a pact? Like, I tell you when things aren't going so hot—if I need help on my homework, or I just want to talk about stuff—"

Dad rubbed his chin. "What's my end of the bargain?" he asked, like it was this important deal he wanted to close.

I thought it over. "You could quit worrying so much about the competition. About winning trophies and stuff. And stop buying everyone presents, unless it's their birthday or Christmas—" I took a deep breath. "And give this treatment thing a decent shot."

Maybe I shouldn't have added that part about the presents, I thought, as a frown crossed his face. In fact, maybe I shouldn't have said anything at all.

Dad looked at me for a long time. I was starting to feel pretty nervous; I wasn't good at talking about stuff, either.

Finally, he cleared his throat. "Where I come from," he said, "guys shake on a deal."

So we shook on it.

By the time Mom came home with the groceries, most of the Oreos were gone, but she didn't seem to mind. While we were cleaning up the kitchen, Mom told me she wasn't happy about what I'd done, but she was glad Ms. Loomis still believed in me.

"Staying after school and being off the team are punishment enough. This time. But you have to promise to clean up your act. Okay, Kyle?"

I nodded. Then she told me there was a kids' group at the counseling place where Dad was going, and some night I might want to come along. I told her I'd think about it.

Brian went, though. I asked him if he liked it, and he grinned and said there were a couple of girls there he wouldn't mind seeing again. Good old Bri.

"Seems like we already painted this section," I said.

I wiped my face and stared at the green trim on the cafeteria wall. It seemed to stretch for miles. "Like maybe a hundred times," I added.

"Who cares?" said Boyd. "All I know is my back's killing me!" He stood up and groaned loudly.

"Take a break?" I suggested. He grunted and we both flopped down on the floor, careful not to lean against the fresh paint. Boyd reached into his pocket and pulled out a lint-covered candy bar. He snapped it in two and tossed half to me. We munched in silence.

Now that my sentence was nearly up, I was almost used to Boyd. But I'd found out a few surprising things. One was that Boyd had a consuming passion in life, and it wasn't basketball. It was hockey.

For an entire month Boyd had done nothing but talk hockey. He talked about his dad, who refereed hockey, and his brothers, who played on some semi-pro level. He explained every nuance of the game. As we plastered the wall with green paint, Boyd told me the name of every team who'd ever won the Stanley Cup. Make that every team who ever made the *finals*. There were about a thousand of them.

Not that it didn't bore me. But I noticed something else: When Boyd babbled about hockey he seemed almost human. (Plus it explained why he threw so many elbows on the court.)

I also learned how Boyd earned his spot on the detention squad: He got caught with one of Joel's answer sheets during a quiz. That one surprised me—I figured the Great Gum-Up had made them mortal enemies. But Pearson looked at things more practically.

"Hey, this beats getting expelled," he said, peering at the green stripe that went all the way around the cafeteria. "That creep Hicks. I should have pounded him when I had the chance."

I considered telling Boyd about cracking Joel's nose. But I didn't want to give him any ideas. Joel was right next door, scrubbing graffiti off the bathroom walls.

In the meantime, Boyd was off the Warriors, and Joel and I were off the Knowledge Bowl team. The school had a fresh coat of paint and a row of scraggly new bushes out front. And I'd had a lot of time to think.

Mostly I thought about Rowena.

We hadn't spoken in a month, since that day in the hall. I tried to tell myself it was her fault for listening to other people's conversations, but I knew that was stupid. I had no one to blame but myself.

Sure enough, Rowena got to be captain of the Knowledge Bowl team, leading our fearless foursome to defeat in the county tryouts. Which just goes to show that being a math genius will only take a person so far.

I dusted off my pants and stood up. "Let's do it," I said, reaching for my paintbrush.

"Nah," he said. "I'm done. Finish it tomorrow."

I shrugged. "Suit yourself." I watched Boyd shamble off to terrorize some seventh-graders. It felt good to know I was finally off Boyd's hit list. Being a member of the same chain gang had its advantages.

I carried the brushes back to the kitchen and rinsed them in the sink. On my way out, I stuck my head in the boys' bathroom. "You through for the day?" I called.

"Almost." Joel's head popped out from under a cubicle. "Want to get something to eat?"

I paused. "No, I've got some studying to do. Anything interesting on the walls?"

"Not really. 'I hate my teacher.' Except he spelled 'teacher' with two E's."

I laughed. "No wonder he hates her!"

Joel rolled his eyes. "Catch you later, Kip." His head disappeared back under the cubicle.

Make that a *lot* later, I thought—Joel's sentence stretched past Christmas. But as long as he steered clear of Boyd, he'd come out okay. Joel was just that kind of guy.

I was starting to figure out that I wasn't. Which didn't stop me from liking Joel. I just didn't want to follow in his footsteps. Or anyone else's, for that matter.

It was a clear fall day, the kind that throws sharp shadows on the sidewalk and makes you forget winter is right around the corner. I tried to remember the last time I'd even noticed the weather.

Probably not since Dad stopped drinking. When I checked the space behind the woodpile, it was empty; after that, I decided not to look anymore. Not because I didn't worry about it, because I did. But you couldn't hold your breath forever.

The bike zoomed effortlessly around the curves. What a honey. I cruised the streets of Wheaton like a two-wheeled astronaut.

No more secrets, no more lies. The pedals pumped in time to the words. No more Pearson, no more Hicks, no more Maxwell dirty tricks!

CHAPTER 20

The house was quiet when I got inside. Even Cindy was nowhere in sight. I went in the kitchen, made myself a thick molasses shake, and drank it down.

Then I stared at my shoes to see if they looked any farther away. Maybe next year I'd take Bri's advice and try out for track. The high school coach might be able to use someone who was light on his feet. Couldn't hurt to ask.

I was fixing another shake when I heard something out back. It was the ring of a hammer striking wood. I paused at the window. Dad stood in the yard, a pile of lumber at his feet.

I finished stirring the milk and took it outside. "Hi," I said, staring at the lumber. "Building something?"

Dad laughed. "That obvious, huh?" He pointed at the blueprint on the picnic table. "Thought I might enclose the patio this winter. Put in some of those solarium windows. It would make a nice studio for your mother."

"Sounds great." I bent over to look at the plans.

"Did you know she was painting for some greeting card outfit?"

I glanced up. "Well . . ."

Dad scratched his head. "She wanted the money to be a surprise. In case my year-end bonus didn't come through. Bonus!" he laughed. "She'll probably be running her own company one of these days."

"Or an art gallery," I suggested.

"Kyle . . ." He was rattling through a can of nails. "Listen—I took that pool back to the store. I don't think there'll be room in the yard now, what with the new plants and the—"

"That's okay, Dad." I grabbed the blueprint. "So, you going to build the deck they show here? That means you'll have to put in a new door, right?"

He nodded and peered down at the plans. "I figured we could put a railing on this side . . ."

I listened to Dad's voice and watched his hands measure out the deck we were going to build. Things were better these days, since he'd started going to meetings. Nothing dramatic like in the movies. Life just seemed more . . . normal.

And even a little boring. That was okay with me. I didn't miss that crummy feeling of suspense every day, waiting for the Stranger to show up. Sometimes boring has a lot going for it.

But I still missed Rowena.

I watched Dad work on his plans. After a while, I went in the house and got my jacket.

The Whipples' house was in an uproar when I got there.

"It's Arnold," Rebecca—or maybe Roxanne—told me

breathlessly. "He was playing with the dog next door and it bit him!"

"You mean he fed it a firecracker and it bit him," I corrected her. She shot me a dirty look and went off to comfort the poor Rat.

Just then, Mrs. Whipple came home from the store, and everybody was busy telling her what happened, and packing Arnold off to get his rabies shots.

"You take care, buddy," I told him as they were carrying him down the steps. "Don't talk to any strange dogs, okay?"

The Rat twisted away from his mom to look at me. He narrowed his eyes. I held my breath, waiting for Arnold to call me a "puke-head."

Instead he brought his finger up and aimed at me. "Bang," he said. But you could tell he meant it in a friendly way.

I figured that was a good sign. I grabbed one of the younger kids. "Where's Rowena?"

The kid screwed up his face—a Whipple family trait. "Out back," he said. "Talkin' to Fenwick."

Taking a deep breath, I headed for the pigeon coop.

She was there, all right, kneeling next to the cage, poking some corn through the mesh.

I cleared my throat loudly.

Nothing. Not so much as a twitch.

"Hey, I heard about Arnold," I called. "Tough break, huh?"

I saw Rowena's back go rigid. Finally her head moved up and down in a stiff nod.

I shoved my hands in my pockets and walked over to the coop. "Want to talk?"

No response. I kneeled down next to her. "If you want, I'll talk and you can just listen. Or the other way around is fine too."

Her head came up, and she looked at me. I withered, but managed to hold my ground.

"You would have passed, Kyle," Rowena said finally. "I just know it! And I kind of hate you for not having the guts to find out." She scowled at me.

I sighed. "Well, I kind of hate you for being right about everything, Rowena. As usual. But I kind of still like you, too, if that makes any sense."

She still looked mad. I backpedaled fast.

"Look, I know I really screwed up. And I think I know why now, and I can basically guarantee that it won't happen again, 'cause I'm a changed guy."

Rowena sucked in her cheeks. "It was a crummy thing to do, Ky-uhl."

"Yes," I agreed. "I was a total, complete jerk."

"But not as big a jerk as that Joel Hicks. Who I was right about all along, incidentally."

"Absolutely." I felt like there was a Slinky in my neck, I was nodding so hard. "One hundred percent correct."

I wasn't sure if she forgave me or not. Instead, Rowena picked up the sack of feed corn and started tossing some into the cage. "I guess you heard how we did at the Knowledge Bowl."

"Pretty good is the way I heard it. Centerville must have

snuck in some rocket scientists disguised as kids."

"They did not, Ky-uhl! We blew it." Her shoulders drooped. "Or rather, I did. You want to know the worst part?"

"Dying to," I said.

"I missed a math question! A dumb little problem about decimals. I mean, I can do decimals in my sleep! I couldn't believe it."

"Hey, nobody's perfect. Not even you, Rowe."

"Well, we could have used some *help*," she said.

We stood next to the coop for a long time, kicking at the gravel. After a moment she glanced at me.

"You look different," she observed.

"Told you. I'm a changed guy. Maybe a little taller, too," I added.

"In one month?" Rowena screwed up her face and squinted at me. "Does that mean you're going to play basketball, Kyle?"

"I was thinking about track. But not until next year. I don't think Coach Simpson's ready for a guy with my rare talents just yet."

Rowena snorted so hard, she almost choked. "Don't forget the genius part," she said.

"I won't, Decimal Brains!"

I could feel the corn swish toward my head before it got there. Just in time I ducked. I swooped down for the sack of feed and grabbed a good handful. We headed out to the yard, lobbing kernels at each other. Rowena's got a pretty good arm, but I can outrun her any day.

But not today, I thought, slowing down to give her time

to aim. Maybe, just this once, I'd let her take her best shot.

Something hard pelted the back of my neck and crept down my shirt.

"Got you that time, Maxwell! Think you're so tough!"

"Tougher than you, Whipple!" I called. "Faster, too. Faster with one foot tied behind my back. Faster *backwards!*"

"We'll see about that," she shrieked. And then we were racing down the driveway, arms and legs bumping into each other, trying to knock each other into the hedge.

When we were both out of breath, I threw myself down in the Whipples' front yard. "So—you want to go to the game on Friday?" I paused. "We're playing Lewistown. It's gonna be a blowout. Could be entertaining."

Rowena gave me a suspicious look.

"It's not a date or something like that?" she asked, this weird, noodly look crawling over her face.

"Nope, Rowena. It's just a really lame basketball game. If it makes you feel any better, my dad's coming too. And no way does he want a date with you!"

I kind of improvised that last part. But it did the trick. Rowena relaxed. She even managed to look kind of annoyed.

"Okay," she said. "I'll go." Then her face got stern and she said, "Have you talked to Celia lately?"

I stared down at the grass. The fact was, I hadn't. We still said hi in the hall, and I got a good look at her in Campbell's class, but that was it. I figured she'd seen me painting the cafeteria during detention. It didn't exactly fill me with pride.

"She hasn't talked to me, either," I muttered.

"She thinks you're mad at her," Rowena pointed out. "I heard her telling Kim. She thinks you're avoiding her."

"Well, maybe I am." I got up and started brushing the leaves off my jacket.

"So maybe you should give her a chance. It wouldn't kill you, Ky-uhl. Like at the game on Friday, just go up to her and say—"

I groaned. "All right! Enough! You win!"

Rowena smirked. Then someone called her name, and she got up and made a beeline for her front porch. I thought about giving her one last blast of feed corn, but it was getting too dark.

Instead, I headed across the street and gave Cindy a whistle. She trotted over to me, and I bent down and ruffled her coat.

"How about it, girl?" I asked Cindy. "You think Dad would be up for seeing the Warriors get the stuffing knocked out of them?"

Cindy barked. I stroked her silky golden ears, but I was picturing Celia's blond hair spilling over her face, and remembering the sparkly barrette sitting in my desk drawer upstairs.

All of a sudden I couldn't wait to tell Dad about the game.